SHADOW ASSIGNMENT

THE SHADOW AGENCY
BOOK 3

CHRISTY BARRITT

Copyright © 2024 by Christy Barritt

All rights reserved.

No part of this book may be reproduced in any form or by any electronic or mechanical means, including information storage and retrieval systems, without written permission from the author, except for the use of brief quotations in a book review.

CHAPTER ONE

SADIE CARRINGTON'S hands trembled as she climbed from her SUV and slammed the door.

She needed to run.

But she couldn't. Not until she talked to Trevor.

He should be here any minute.

She would tell him everything—including why she had blood on her hands.

She glanced down and saw the red streaks again.

Panic threatened to consume her.

She couldn't let the panic win.

She couldn't lose it right now. She had to hold herself together for a little while longer.

This would have all been easier if she'd stuck to the plan—a plan that hadn't included falling for Trevor McGrath.

Everything had been one mistake after another.

Now she needed to make things right.

Sadie paused near her Bronco and surveyed the parking lot.

No one else was at the small, secluded beach located on Lake Michigan. Its privacy was part of the reason she liked it here.

She blew out a long breath as she rehearsed what she would say.

She could do this.

Sadie looked at her palms again, and her breath caught.

She had to wash her hands. Get the blood off.

She could run to the lake and rinse them there.

But would she have time?

Her phone buzzed. She pulled it from her pocket and glanced at the screen.

Trevor.

She quickly read the message.

> Running a few minutes late. Can't wait to see you.

She shoved the phone back into the pocket of her shorts. She hoped he would get there soon.

The more time that passed, the more she feared she might change her mind.

But she didn't want to leave him wondering.

She hadn't known Trevor long, but she cared too

much to do that to him. She cared enough to risk everything.

She started across the lot to the walkover. The sounds of the lake's rolling waves grew louder as she approached the beach.

Her oversized bag cut into her shoulder. She should have parked closer to the beach, but she liked her corner spot. It was shaded and, at first glance, easy to miss her vehicle there in the shadows. That made the space perfect.

Sadie readjusted her bag then stopped and turned when she heard a car pull into the lot.

She glanced at the dark sedan with tinted windows.

Not Trevor.

Great. Someone else was here.

Disappointment gripped her. She needed privacy right now. The fewer people who were around, the better.

Then the engine revved as the driver headed toward her.

She froze, contemplating backing up to the sidewalk.

But the driver didn't slow.

Instead, he gunned the engine, and the vehicle accelerated at an alarming speed.

It charged straight toward her.

Panic kicked into gear.

Sadie needed to move.

She might not be able to outrun the vehicle.

But she would try.

With a piercing scream, Sadie dropped the beach bag, turned on her heel, and sprinted toward the dune in the distance.

Trevor McGrath glanced at the beautiful coast to his right as he drove his truck along the shore.

He'd always thought of beaches as being more of an East Coast/West Coast thing. But Michigan had proven him wrong. The shorelines here were gorgeous with sparkling water, soft sand, and a smattering of green trees gathered on gently sloping hills like fans assembled on bleachers.

But it wasn't the beach that really had him excited.

It was seeing Sadie.

He already had the whole day planned for them.

He'd packed a picnic lunch. An oversized beach blanket. He even brought a frisbee for them to toss around.

Today would be fantastic.

The only unfortunate part was that he had to keep his budding relationship with Sadie a secret.

He hated the fact that seeing her was so cloak-

and-dagger. But his boss, Alan Larchmont, didn't approve of romantic entanglements. Not that there weren't exceptions. Two of his colleagues were now in successful relationships, so it was possible to change the man's mind.

Trevor didn't want to go through the headache of trying to convince Larchmont that he deserved a life outside of work. Not yet. It wasn't that Sadie wasn't worth it.

She was *absolutely* worth it.

But Trevor needed to see where the two of them were going before he took those steps.

That was why he hadn't told anyone what he was doing. Why he'd continued to see her in such a secluded location. He didn't want anything to burst the bubble around their budding romance. If he had his way, he'd keep it like this for as long as possible.

Beaches stretched up and down Michigan's coast, some busier than others.

But this beach—the one where he and Sadie had initially met—was a hidden gem. Though it was maintained by the state and had a decent-sized parking lot, it wasn't considered a tourist hotspot.

He wasn't complaining. Having a slice of paradise to share with Sadie was something he'd take any day.

He turned off the main road and toward the parking area where he and Sadie were meeting.

As he did, he spotted two vehicles in the lot.

One was parked in the corner of the lot—Sadie's Bronco.

The other was a dark sedan, and it was racing across the lot . . . toward a woman.

His lungs froze.

Not just any woman.

The driver charged toward . . . Sadie.

CHAPTER TWO

POWERLESS TO DO ANYTHING, Trevor watched as Sadie darted away.

But it was too late.

She couldn't outrun the car.

The sedan rammed into her, and she flew through the air.

She landed in the sand in a sickening heap.

The car peeled away, headed toward the exit on the other side of the lot.

Trevor had to make a quick decision: follow the car and bring the person who'd done this to justice. Or check on Sadie.

He pulled up beside Sadie's limp form, threw his truck into Park, and hopped out. Before he even reached her, he dialed 911. He knew by seeing the force of the impact that she would need more help than he could give.

She needed medical attention.

Plus, the police would need to investigate the scene and track down whoever had done this.

He fell to his knees on the ground beside her and quickly scanned her. Saw her closed eyes. Her unmoving body.

"Sadie." He touched her arm. "Can you hear me?"

She didn't stir.

Trevor pressed his finger against her neck.

She had a pulse.

Relief rushed through him.

Then he searched for signs of any broken bones and ran his hands gently along her arms, legs, and ribs. He didn't feel anything bulging out of place.

His gaze stopped at her arm.

A red trickle ran down her forearm. Stained her hands.

Was that . . . blood?

Was it *her* blood?

He checked her again but didn't see anywhere she might be bleeding. Besides, the blood was . . . dry.

Old.

What sense did that make?

He turned back to Sadie. "Sadie, it's me. Everything's going to be okay." Trevor gently squeezed her hand. "The ambulance is on its way. Help will be here soon."

Again, no response.

Who would have done this? Sadie was one of the sweetest women he'd ever met. She didn't seem like the type to have a single enemy.

Then another thought hit.

Could one of *his* enemies have done this?

Trevor shook the thought off. He'd been careful.

No one knew where he was. He hadn't been followed. He'd even left his work phone at home in favor of a burner phone so he couldn't be traced.

Due to his line of work, he often checked his vehicle to make sure no trackers had been planted on it. He'd chosen an old-school truck, one without all the bells and whistles that came with having electronic control units—which were basically miniature computers that could be remotely manipulated.

He'd picked this truck on purpose.

He didn't want anyone to hack into his vehicle's electronics and sabotage anything.

Because of his career, he had to be careful.

Sirens began to wail in the distance.

Help would be here soon.

Trevor scanned the ground. Sadie's beach bag lay in the sand several feet away. Her car keys, sunscreen, and a bottle of water were scattered around it. A piece of paper fluttered in the wind, about to be carried away with the breeze.

He snatched it up and saw a list of numbers.

Quickly, he shoved the paper in his pocket.

He turned back to Sadie and prayed that the EMTs wouldn't be too late.

———

For the past hour, Trevor had paced the hospital hallway as he waited to hear an update on Sadie.

So far, there had been nothing.

Worst-case scenarios pummeled him. Scenarios where Sadie didn't wake up. Scenarios where something was seriously wrong, something he hadn't been able to spot. Brain bleeds. Paralysis. Internal bleeding.

The longer he waited, the longer the list became.

Plus, there were those things he couldn't explain.

Things like the dried blood.

Blood no one else would ever see.

Using a water bottle and a beach towel, he had gently washed the stains from her hands. Then he'd stashed the towel in his truck out of sight.

The blood just seemed so . . . incriminating. He didn't want the police asking too many questions.

He supposed it was his way of protecting Sadie. He hoped he didn't regret it.

How could he? If he hadn't been five minutes late, then none of this would have happened. He would have been there to keep her safe.

If only he could turn back time. His jaw hardened when he realized his failure.

He paused from his pacing and shoved a hand into his pocket. A paper scratched his skin.

The paper he'd found near Sadie's beach bag . . .

He hadn't really looked at it earlier.

He opened it and smoothed the wrinkles before studying the handwritten note. He recognized the handwriting as Sadie's.

He squinted. It was a series of numbers. There didn't seem to be rhyme or reason to them, however. They were different lengths, no numerical order.

Why would Sadie have this with her? Was it something from work?

They'd made a deal when they met each other that they wouldn't ask too many personal questions —nothing about work specifically. The arrangement had seemed perfect.

But now he wished he knew more. He hadn't even snooped and researched her on his own. In fact, he kind of liked not knowing.

As he stood beside the door to Sadie's room, a voice drifted out. It sounded like the doctor was talking to the nurse.

"Remarkably, there are no broken bones," the

man said. "Just some bruises and cuts. In that regard, she's very lucky."

Relief swept through Trevor.

"However, there *is* the matter of her head injury. We'll need to carefully monitor her."

Unease sloshed inside Trevor.

Head injuries were serious matters, namely because of the possibility of brain damage.

As footsteps came closer, Trevor stepped back, trying not to make it obvious he'd been eavesdropping.

A moment later, a fiftyish man with a stocky build, honey-blond hair cut close, and a square face stepped into the hallway.

His gaze found Trevor. "You're the man who found our hit-and-run victim?"

Trevor paused from pacing and swallowed hard before nodding. "I am. Trevor McGrath. How is she?"

"I'm Dr. Conroy." The man extended his arm for a handshake. "Unfortunately, she's still not awake."

"I'm sorry to hear that." Trevor shook hands with the man and then shifted. "I know this might be an unusual request, but could I see her?"

Dr. Conroy studied him again.

As far as the man knew, Trevor was a stranger.

He hated not telling the whole truth. But he needed to keep his relationship with Sadie quiet. Any hint of them knowing each other would raise questions.

Questions Trevor may not be able to answer, especially since he and Sadie weren't supposed to be together. If people became too curious, Trevor's true identity could come into question.

He needed to exist purely as a ghost.

"The nurse is in there with her now," Dr. Conroy finally said. "If you'd like to step inside a moment, you're welcome to. But she'll need her rest. The police are on their way. As soon as she's speaking again, they'll want to question her."

"Of course."

An unusual rush of jitters swept through Trevor as he carefully pushed open the door.

Sadie lay in the hospital bed, a white sheet tucked around her. Her bathing suit and coverup were gone in favor of a blue hospital gown.

Her dark hair lay in waves around her face, and her eyes were closed.

A middle-aged nurse with blonde hair, who introduced herself as Kate, adjusted the IV in Sadie's arm, offering a quick glance and smile to Trevor as she continued to work.

Trevor paced to the other side of the bed and stared at Sadie.

He wanted to reach out and touch her. To sweep her hair away from her face. To tell her how sorry he was about everything that happened. How he was sorry he was late.

But he didn't do any of that. They'd been on only four dates. It seemed too soon.

At that thought, Sadie's eyelids fluttered. Then fluttered again.

Her head twitched.

Her lips pressed together as if the movements had caused her discomfort.

Trevor's lungs squeezed as he waited for whatever she would do next.

Her eyes opened.

She looked straight ahead.

Then at him.

But her gaze didn't linger on him long.

Instead, panic filled the depths of her eyes. "Where am I?"

"It's okay, Sadie. You're at the hospital." Nurse Kate pressed a hand against her shoulder and spoke in soft but firm tones. "We've been waiting for you to wake up."

"The hospital?" Her eyes widened.

"You were in a car accident." Trevor figured that might be a little easier to swallow than telling her she'd been hit by a car.

Her gaze jerked from the nurse to Trevor.

Then she asked, "Who are you?"

Trevor's heart pounded like a drum in his ears. Had she . . . lost her memory?

CHAPTER
THREE

SADIE WANTED to grab the wires and tubes connected to her, jerk them away from her body, and run.

She tried to sit up, but the nurse gently pressed her back in bed. "You need to lie still. Your body has just been through a traumatic event."

A traumatic event?

She held up her hands and studied them. Then she touched her face. Moved her legs.

She was stiff and sore. Had cuts and bruises. But other than that . . .

The man beside her said she was in a car accident.

Then why didn't she have anything other than minor abrasions? Or maybe she did. Maybe she just couldn't see or feel anything else yet.

She tried to make sense of things—but it was useless.

The man beside her leaned closer, his eyes narrow with concern. "Do you remember what happened?"

She studied his face. Studied the chiseled features of his cheekbones and nose. His blond hair. His trim, muscular build.

The man was handsome. Probably in his early thirties with an air of mystery about him.

Why was he in the room with her? He didn't appear to be a doctor. So who was he? A detective maybe?

Why couldn't she remember?

She squeezed her eyes shut, trying to dredge up some type of recollection.

But her mind only contained blank spaces.

How could that be?

Did she even know her name? Had the nurse called her Sadie?

She searched her thoughts again, waiting for them to stop somewhere.

They didn't.

More panic welled inside her.

She sucked in a breath and opened her eyes again.

"Who am I?" The question came out as a whisper.

The man's eyes widened.

He looked at the nurse, who exchanged a worried glance with him.

"You don't recall your name?" Nurse Kate peered at her with concern in her gaze.

"I . . . I don't remember anything. Nothing at all." Nausea grew in her gut.

The man and woman exchanged another worried glance.

"Your name is Sadie Carrington, and you're thirty-three years old," the nurse finally said. "That's what your driver's license says. Does that ring any bells?"

Sadie shook her head, which she instantly regretted as a throb began.

Bad idea. She couldn't move her head anymore. She must have hit it.

Her gaze went back to the man. "Who are you?"

Something strange passed through the man's gaze. "I'm Trevor McGrath."

Before he could say any more, the nurse jumped in. "He's the man who found you in the parking lot and called 911."

"In the parking lot?" Sadie tried to put the pieces together. "After my car accident?"

"It was a car accident, I *suppose*," the nurse said. "But you were a pedestrian, and you were hit by a car."

"What?" Her voice wavered with uncertainty. "Who hit me? What happened?"

"We're still trying to figure all that out," Nurse

Kate said. "The doctor will be back in a moment and maybe he can explain more."

A sense of despair swelled inside her.

Sadie Carrington.

The name didn't sound familiar.

No new memories had emerged. Only more blank spaces.

What did this mean? Was anyone out there looking for her right now? Family? Friends? A husband or a significant other?

Where would Sadie even go when she left here? Did she have a house or an apartment? Could she drive?

The uncertainties quickly began to rip away at her, and tears rolled down her cheeks.

Trevor opened his mouth to offer some kind of assurance to Sadie. But there were no words to make this better. Instead, he pressed his lips together as regret filled him.

He wanted to reach for her. To offer her some comfort. To wipe those tears away.

But he didn't.

Besides, she didn't remember him. Doing any of those things would be awkward and possibly unwelcome.

He studied her face another moment, looking for any signs her memories were slowly returning.

There was nothing, only confusion and panic.

Sadie truly didn't remember anything.

Dr. Conroy rushed into the room. He quickly introduced himself to Sadie, explained how long she'd been there, and gave a recap of what they'd found. As he spoke, he took a light from his pocket and shone it into each of her eyes. Then he listened to her heart.

None of those facts seemed to comfort Sadie. Instead, her eyes widened even more as quiet tears rolled down her cheeks.

"I know you've been through a lot." The doctor paused, his expression growing grim. "We'll send Dr. Evans, the hospital psychologist, to talk to you about your amnesia."

"Amnesia?" Sadie's voice pitched higher. "How long will it last? Will I ever regain my memories?"

The doctor's expression remained pinched. "Dr. Evans should be able to tell you more. I'll also send in a referral to a neurologist. In most cases, these memory issues are simply post-traumatic amnesia that can last a few minutes to several weeks or months."

"And in other cases?" Her throat burned as the question left her lips.

His frown deepened. "Other times these things

can have more long-lasting effects. But that's generally not the case, so let's not think in worst-case scenarios quite yet."

Trevor swallowed hard. In other words, sometimes people never regained their memories.

Silence stretched as Sadie seemed to let that sink in.

Finally, she cleared her throat, her gaze focusing back on the doctor. "How long will I stay here?"

"You'll stay here as long as you need to." Dr. Conroy patted her hand. "Leaving is the last thing you should worry about right now. We just need to work on getting you back on track."

Sadie nodded quickly before scrunching her eyes and reaching for her temple.

"With your head trauma, you should move slowly," the doctor said. "The good news is you seem healthy otherwise. But we *do* need to monitor you. In the meantime, a detective is on his way up to talk to you. Is that okay?"

"I guess so." Her voice sounded soft and uncertain, however. "Maybe the police can tell me more."

Just then, Trevor's phone buzzed—his burner phone.

Who would be texting him? Sadie was the only one he'd given this number to—and Sadie clearly wasn't the one texting him right now.

His shoulders tightened as he pulled the device from his pocket.

Right away, he recognized the number on his screen.

Larchmont.

How did his boss even get this number?

> Meet me in the hallway.

The hallway? Was he referring to the hallway outside this room?

Trevor's chest muscles pulled taut.

He should have known better than to think he could keep secrets from his boss. Larchmont was the master of subterfuge, often called the All-Knowing One by Trevor's colleagues.

Now Trevor would need to face the consequences of his choices.

But that didn't matter at the moment.

Only Sadie.

Who had done this to her? Why did she have blood on her hands and arm? And what was up with that list of numbers he'd found near her bag?

CHAPTER
FOUR

TREVOR EXCUSED HIMSELF, hoping he wasn't losing the opportunity to stay close to Sadie. Who knew if he would be allowed back in that room? Another nurse could come on shift and refuse to let him in.

But if Larchmont truly was outside, he couldn't avoid the man.

Trevor stepped into the hallway and spotted someone standing against the wall directly across from him.

His stomach sank.

Alan Larchmont.

The sixty-something man had a shock of white hair and a tall, thin, muscular frame. His distinguished features masked the fact he was a trained assassin. He relied on logic, not emotion, in nearly every situation.

Those facts had served him well in his career. But it didn't make him any easier to deal with.

"Trevor." Larchmont's voice sounded as gruff as always. "Let's take a walk."

"I prefer not to get too far away." Trevor bristled, preparing himself for an argument. "Someone made an attempt on Sadie's life. Who's to say they won't try again?"

Larchmont didn't deny that Sadie could still be in danger, but irritation flickered in his gaze as if he didn't appreciate the insubordination. "Fine. Let's walk to the end of the hall. You can still see her room, but we'll have more privacy."

Trevor agreed, and they paced toward the exit door. As they paused, Trevor kept himself angled to see Sadie's room.

"This is my time off. How did you find me?" He glanced back at Larchmont, not able to hide his anger at the fact he'd been tracked.

Larchmont remained unapologetic. "I make it my business to keep tabs on all my guys."

Alan Larchmont ran the Shadow Agency, a top-secret organization staffed by former members of a clandestine government military experiment. Larchmont had been their fearless leader while they were enlisted. When he retired, he'd recruited each of them to join him.

They did work no one else wanted to do. Work where they needed to remain nameless and faceless. Work where their ability to slip in and later disappear was essential.

"This is a private matter." Trevor was unwilling to concede.

He'd given everything to the government and then to the Shadow Agency. He'd given so much that he'd nearly forgotten who he was. What kinds of food he liked. He had no idea what kind of vacations he'd like to go on one day. Had no dreams of ever having a life outside the job.

Then he'd realized how meaningless that felt, and he'd decided to make some changes.

Meeting Sadie had sealed the deal.

That evening, he'd been at the beach watching the sunset. No one else was there—just the way he liked it.

Then Sadie arrived, looking equally disappointed to have to share the shore.

When a sudden wind had sent her hat flying across the beach, Trevor had retrieved it. They'd struck up a conversation, and one thing led to another.

Trevor had asked her out to dinner that evening, and she'd said yes.

"In this line of work, *nothing* is private." Larchmont scowled. "Private matters are liabilities."

"I deserve a life outside the Shadow Agency."

Larchmont's expression remained hard. "You knew what you were signing up for."

Each of his colleagues *officially* knew what they were getting into when they joined. But after years of living unconnected, almost nomadic lives, many of them were becoming restless. Many were wanting more than what they'd found after giving their lives to an agency that may or may not care about them.

"So you found out I bought a burner phone and was seeing Sadie Carrington." Trevor's jaw tightened as he said the words, but he tried to set his emotions aside.

Larchmont had come here for a reason. Otherwise, they could have simply had this conversation when he got back into the office in Detroit. "That's correct."

"I thought you were still in Wyoming." That was the last Trevor had heard.

"I'm wherever I need to be."

Trevor didn't like the sound of that. He'd had reservations about the man for a while, but after his last case, he had even more.

Larchmont was hiding something. Trevor was sure of it.

Recently, one of their suspects had been on the

verge of sharing a secret when Larchmont had pulled the trigger and silenced the woman. Larchmont had said it was to protect his agents because their suspect was about to kill them all.

But Trevor wasn't so sure.

"So why are you here?" Trevor crossed his arms over his chest as he waited for his boss to respond.

"I need you to stay close to Sadie."

Trevor blinked. That wasn't what he'd expected to hear.

"You mean I can tell her who I really am?" he clarified.

Larchmont grimaced. "No."

Trevor shook his head, trying to make sense of what his boss was telling him. "Then what are you talking about?"

"Sadie Carrington may have been sent by one of our enemies to befriend you."

Sadie glanced at her arm and squinted.

She held it closer and observed a faint outline of red.

What was that?

It almost looked like . . . blood.

But her IV was in the opposite arm. From all appearances, she hadn't cut herself.

So why . . . ?

What had she been doing at the beach? Had she been about to meet someone?

Was there some type of trouble brewing in her life that had suddenly disappeared from her memory?

Her thoughts raced but went nowhere. Unless a friend or a coworker or a family member came forward with information, she was going to flounder in a sea of the unknown right now.

Her gaze drifted to the window beside her bed. She had a view of the front of the hospital and everyone coming and going.

A man walking toward the hospital entrance caught her eye.

Her lungs tightened at the sight of him.

Why? What was it about that man wearing the black leather jacket and dark jeans that caused her to feel such sudden panic?

Did she know him?

"Everything okay?" Nurse Kate peered at her. "Your heart rate just kicked up a notch."

She continued to watch the man as he disappeared into the hospital.

Was he coming to see her?

Her heart continued to pump harder, faster.

"Sadie?"

With the man now gone and out of sight, she jerked her head back toward the nurse.

The woman repeated her question. "Is everything okay?"

What should she say? Sadie wasn't sure. Yet something internal told her not to mention that man.

But why? It didn't make sense.

"I think I'm just tired," Sadie finally murmured. "This is . . . a lot."

"I can only imagine. I'm going to let you get your rest in a second."

Sadie nodded. "The man that was in here—the one who found me? Trevor. Is he outside the room or did he leave?"

"Let me look for you."

The nurse cracked the door open just slightly before stepping back toward Sadie. "He's still there. Did you want to see him?"

"No, I am okay. But would you stay in here with me for a few more minutes? I just don't want to be alone right now."

Sadie held her breath, fearing that the nurse would refuse her. Certainly, the woman had other patients she needed to see.

Instead, the nurse smiled kindly and nodded. "Yes, I'd be happy to stay a little while longer."

Sadie wanted to breathe a sigh of relief.

But she couldn't stop thinking about that man outside and why he might be here at the hospital. Why did seeing him cause her anxiety to ratchet?

Why did her fear—her fight-or-flight instincts—kick in? And why did she have an impending feeling that he was headed to her room and that her life could be on the line?

It made no sense.

Yet somehow, it felt like the truth.

CHAPTER
FIVE

TREVOR MUST NOT HAVE HEARD Larchmont correctly. But his boss's expression remained stony, without the slightest trace of humor.

One of our enemies . . .

That would be hard to narrow down. Trevor and his colleagues had a long list of adversaries in their line of work.

Any of them might want to destroy Trevor, his colleagues, and/or the agency they worked for.

"You can't be serious," Trevor finally muttered. Why would Larchmont ever think that?

"I'm dead serious. Her past doesn't check out."

"What does that even mean?" Was this a mind game Larchmont was playing on him? His boss's way of manipulating the situation?

"The real Sadie Carrington died in a car accident

four years ago. The woman you befriended assumed her identity."

Trevor narrowed his eyes. "Tell me more."

"I don't know this woman's true identity yet, but she's not the accountant she claims to be. That's where you come in. You need to get close to her and find out who she really is. We need to know the truth."

Trevor could see his boss's point. If enemies wanted inside information on the Shadow Agency, he and his colleagues needed to know who would go to such desperate measures and why.

But personal and professional lines had intermingled, leaving things even more complicated than usual.

"If Sadie has an assumed identity, then she has a good reason for it," Trevor finally said.

"Not in our line of work."

Trevor opened his mouth to dispute what Larchmont said, but he couldn't. His boss was right.

"She lost her memory," Trevor said instead.

His eyes widened. He hadn't known that yet.

"Hopefully, she'll regain it," Larchmont said. "When she does, you need to find out what she knows."

Trevor clamped his mouth shut, not liking the thought of any of this.

"In the meantime, don't tell her you knew each other before," Larchmont added.

Trevor's eyes widened at the audacity of his boss's words. "Wouldn't it be easier to get close to her if she knows about our prior relationship?"

Larchmont's gaze locked with his. "Not knowing her beforehand makes you less of a liability if things go south or if the feds get involved."

"The feds?" Trevor's voice rose in surprise.

"If it turns out Sadie is trying to get classified information from you about your time in the military, you'll want to distance yourself from her. As it stands right now, you just met because you saved her life. Get to know her, but keep her at arm's length if you know what I mean."

Trevor's shoulders ached as he tried to comprehend everything Larchmont had said.

This couldn't be happening.

He didn't want to be in this position.

Yet, on the other hand, if Larchmont's words were true, maybe Trevor *should* put personal distance between himself and Sadie.

Then another thought hit him: what if Sadie had been using him this whole time?

He couldn't marry the image he had of Sadie with the image of the woman who might be a backstabber.

But the best operatives were great at what they did—great at subterfuge.

And if Sadie Carrington wasn't even her real name . . . then who was she?

Could Trevor really have been this naive? It wasn't usually a word used to describe him. He'd always been so cautious. So on edge. So unwilling to let his guard down.

But Sadie had been different.

He'd allowed her to slip past his defenses.

Maybe that had been his first mistake.

Still, the situation Larchmont had presented him with felt impossible.

His boss wanted him to get close to Sadie without sharing that the two of them had been dating. Trevor had to get close to her but not too close. Close enough to find out information but not close enough to be affiliated with her.

That seemed like the most torturous assignment he might ever receive.

"How am I supposed to do any of this?" Trevor finally dragged his gaze back to Larchmont.

"Someone tried to kill her." Larchmont sounded as if he'd just been waiting for Trevor to ask. "She'll need someone to stay close and keep her safe. She knows you found her and called 911, so she'll already have a measure of trust with you. Tell her you work for a private security group. Everyone will think you were in the right place at the right time for the job. It will be a win-win."

Trevor thought about Larchmont's idea a moment and sighed. As he chewed on the plan, he glanced down the hallway.

A man had started around the corner but paused when he saw Trevor.

The next instant, the man turned and took off in a run.

Wasting no time, Trevor darted after him.

As Trevor rounded the corner, he saw the man was already gone.

What? How could this guy have disappeared so quickly?

He pushed himself forward, still searching for the man.

A flash of movement caught his eye.

It was him. The runner.

He'd ducked into the stairwell.

Trevor hurried after him, not wanting to make a scene but not wanting the guy to get away either.

A food service worker pushing a cart full of dinner trays appeared in front of him.

Trevor stopped so quickly his shoes squeaked. But he didn't collide with the cart.

"Excuse me!" he yelled.

The woman scowled as he hurried past.

The diversion had taken entirely too much time.

Trevor reached the stairwell and paused.

Up or down?

He listened for footsteps.

Down, he decided.

He hurried to the first floor and burst out the doors.

A bustling lobby greeted him.

He scanned everyone there but saw no one suspicious. No one was running or looking over their shoulder.

Then he noticed the trashcan beside him and saw something black poking out.

He grabbed it and frowned.

The black jacket and hat. The man had ditched his outerwear.

Trevor glanced at the people around him.

The runner could be anyone in this crowd. But, most likely, the man was now gone.

Trevor's jaw tightened in frustration.

Who had that been? Was Larchmont right? Was one of their enemies targeting the team? Was Sadie collateral damage? Or was she an enemy herself?

If so, it would take a while to narrow down the culprit. There were too many to count.

Could it be Jovi Casanova, the power-hungry rebel leader who'd tried to overthrow an entire government in eastern Europe?

William Burke, the arms dealer?

Johnson Gwen, the Ponzi scheme guru?

Of course, this was the area where he'd taken down Frederick Moreau, a drug trafficker. But Frederick was now behind bars—for life.

Trevor picked up the jacket and hat. He'd give it to Larchmont to be tested. Maybe there would be some DNA or fingerprints on the material.

For now, he needed to get back to Sadie.

Or whoever she really was.

But he knew this was far from over.

Sadie had to get a grip.

Falling apart right now wasn't an option.

The man she'd seen outside . . . he hadn't appeared in her room. Maybe he hadn't come here to harm her. Maybe her brain was just going haywire.

She tried to concentrate instead on what she did know.

She drew in a deep gulp of air, trying to calm her breathing.

She'd been told her name. Sadie Carrington.

She knew she had a head injury she would need to be supervised for.

She knew she was at the hospital in Traverse City, Michigan.

None of that truly felt like enough, however.

A knock sounded at the door, and a fiftyish man wearing an ill-fitting suit stepped into the room. He was tall and thin with a thick brown mustache and a bland demeanor that matched his pasty skin.

"Detective Bennett with the Traverse City Police Department." He moved his jacket aside to show her the badge at his waist. "I hope I'm not here at a bad time."

"Time seems irrelevant right now."

He paused beside her bed. "Understandable. I need to ask you some questions."

"It's going to be hard for me to answer considering I don't remember anything. They said a car hit me. The man who found me . . . maybe he saw something. Can he come in while we talk?"

It was the strangest thing. There was no reason why Trevor should bring Sadie any semblance of comfort. She didn't even know him.

From what she understood, he was simply a stranger who'd arrived at the beach at the same time she did.

But his eyes seemed kind.

Maybe there was something else he could offer. Or maybe she was just reaching for anything that might bring her some balance. Maybe that man was the only thing she really knew right now—even though she didn't really know him.

"If you're comfortable with him being here, I could talk to you both at the same time," Detective Bennett continued. "Especially because you say you don't remember anything until waking up here at the hospital."

Sadie started to nod, but then remembered the pain that had caused last time. Instead, she responded in a raspy voice. "I said that because it's true. Apparently, I have amnesia."

Detective Bennett stepped into the hallway and said something to someone out of sight. A moment later, the man who'd introduced himself as Trevor strode inside.

He walked to the opposite side of the bed, his hands jammed into the pockets of the zip-up sweatshirt he had on over his pale-blue swim trunks.

Why was there a thin sheen of sweat across his forehead, almost as if he'd been exercising or something?

She tucked the observation away.

"You wanted to see me?" The man's voice sounded tight as he glanced at the detective.

"We're trying to form a timeline and put together a better picture of what happened," Bennett said. "Maybe you can fill in some blanks."

"Whatever I can do. I just can't believe someone did this and drove away. They need to be found and brought to justice. Ms. Carrington could have been killed."

"That's why I'm here," Detective Bennett said. "Tell me what happened from your perspective."

Sadie listened as Trevor recounted his side of the story.

He told the detective about how he'd pulled into the beach parking lot. Had seen a dark-colored sedan charging toward a woman who was running away—but not fast enough.

How the driver had hit her and then squealed away.

Trevor said he wanted to go after the other vehicle, but he knew Sadie needed medical help. However, he did get a license plate number, and he rattled it off to the detective.

Bennett jotted it down. He'd jotted a lot of things down.

He picked up the cell phone near her bed and asked for her permission to look through it. She agreed. Thankfully, the cell had been tucked into the pocket of her jean shorts and not ruined during the accident.

The detective tapped the screen and then frowned.

More concern pulsed through Sadie as she watched his reaction. "What is it?"

"You don't have a passcode or any saved contacts."

She blinked. "What?"

She wasn't sure about the passcode. But didn't everyone have at least a few contacts in their phone?

"What about outgoing calls or text messages?" Her mind continued to race.

"There's just one text that says: Running a few minutes late. Can't wait to see you." Detective Bennett studied her face. "You have no recollection of who may have sent that?"

"None. And there's no one on my contact list who can come to fill me in on the details of my life. . ."

"I'd ask if you had any enemies, but I guess you don't know that either." The detective grimaced as if the words had slipped out unchecked. "My apologies."

"You're right. I don't remember." Yet Sadie didn't feel as if she had enemies.

Could her gut remember things her brain could not?

She had no idea.

An image of the man she'd seen outside filled her mind again. She couldn't stop thinking about him, thinking about her visceral reaction to seeing him.

She needed to figure out what that meant.

"Are you going to see what you can find out about me? Run a background check maybe? I should have a birth certificate or doctor's records somewhere. Maybe the IRS could tell you where I work?"

"Of course, we'll see what we can do. If it makes you feel better, there's no Sadie Carrington in the system down at the station. You don't have a police record. That was one of the first things we checked. We'd like to run your prints also."

"That's fine. Whatever you need." She swallowed hard. "Maybe if you can find the man who hit me and left me to die, then you can find some answers." It was the only thing that made sense to her now. But just how possible would that be? What if they never found this guy?

"That's exactly what I'm hoping to do." Bennett's voice left no room for doubt. "I'll be in touch. We're going to figure out what happened and who you are exactly."

"Okay," Sadie said. "That sounds great."

But a new thought hit her: What if she didn't like what the detective found out? What if there were parts of her life she was better off not knowing?

She swallowed hard as she tried to push those questions aside.

The nurse stepped closer and started to change the fluid going into her IV. Then she paused and squinted. "This can't be right."

"What's wrong?" Bennett asked.

"The orders say to give her this dextrose solution,

but I can't do that with a head injury. It would practically be a death wish." She swung her head back and forth. "This could lead to a cerebral edema."

"Who wrote the order?" Bennett's scowl grew deeper.

"It says Dr. Conroy, but he would never do something like this." Nurse Kate shook her head again as if truly perplexed.

Trevor stepped closer, his jaw visibly hardened and his hands on his hips. "If not Dr. Conroy, then who?"

Nurse Kate frowned. "I'm not sure what's going on. I need to figure that out."

CHAPTER
SIX

TREVOR'S THOUGHTS RACED.

Someone had altered Sadie's medical treatment plan. Based on what he'd put together, that couldn't have been an accident.

Someone had tried to kill Sadie in the parking lot. When that didn't work, they'd come up with a Plan B.

He remembered the man he'd chased. Could he have done this?

He wasn't sure if the guy would have had time.

What he did know was that Detective Bennett must have been getting off the elevator just as Trevor flew down the stairway chasing that man. Their paths had almost crossed, which might have raised some questions.

He turned back to the current situation.

From Trevor's understanding, if that dextrose had been administered, it could have done major damage after Sadie's head injury.

His gut tightened as he realized this was far from being over.

"I need to talk to the doctor," Bennett barked.

"Of course. I'll go get him now." The nurse scurried from the room, still appearing flustered.

Trevor shifted, feeling awkward as he stood there with Sadie and Detective Bennett.

He wanted to step into the situation and take over. To bark out orders. To demand to see security footage from the hospital. To talk to the doctor himself. To ask the police to station someone outside Sadie's room twenty-four/seven.

But Trevor knew he couldn't do that. It would be too aggressive, make this seem too personal.

Even more thoughts ran through his mind.

Could Sadie really have been getting to know him with ulterior motives? Had their initial meeting been orchestrated? Could she work for an enemy of the US?

Trevor found it hard to believe. She'd given no indication of deceit.

The opposite, really.

She'd seemed authentic and genuine—something rare and refreshing in his world. It was part of the reason he'd been so drawn to her.

He wasn't sure how he would navigate his way through this.

The only good news was that he'd sent that text Bennett had found.

But why had she used a burner with no other contacts?

That detail only seemed to prove Larchmont's theory.

Detective Bennett turned toward Trevor as they waited for the nurse to return. "What do you do for a living, Mr. McGrath?"

"I work in private security," Trevor answered.

"You mean like . . . cyber security or something?" Sadie stared up at him.

"I'm a bodyguard, actually."

"Do you work nearby?" A hint of caution edged the detective's voice. "I don't recall seeing you around."

"I work for Stealth Tech, a national company." Trevor used a cover name for the organization, knowing Larchmont had already covered all the bases as far as setting up an online profile, complete with references and testimonials. "I was in the area having a little downtime when I saw what happened to Ms. Carrington."

"I see."

But Trevor didn't like the way the detective eyed

him. The man was suspicious and could be a problem. Trevor needed to try to stay on his good side.

"So you're really a bodyguard?" Sadie suddenly said. "Can I hire you?"

Trevor hesitated as he remembered what Larchmont had said. He hated to deceive Sadie any more than he already had. But this *was* the perfect opportunity.

"Before you say no . . ." She clearly took his silence as a rejection. "I mean, I realize I don't know for sure how I can pay you. But certainly, I have some money."

"I'm not worried about money."

"Oh, wait . . ." She frowned. "You said you were here on vacation, didn't you? I'm sure you probably don't want to work."

Trevor shook his head again, realizing he was really botching this up. "It's not that either. I guess I'm still just trying to process everything. I have a few more days in town, so if you need my assistance, I'd be happy to provide it." He glanced at Detective Bennett. "Do you think that's a good idea?"

Detective Bennett nodded. "Actually, it is. Someone tried to run her over. Since she was the only one in the parking lot, we can only assume she was targeted. Once whoever is responsible figures out they weren't successful, there's a chance they'll try again. That very well could be what happened with the mixed-up medicine as well. Someone could have hacked the system."

Trevor knew that was true. He'd already thought about it.

But that didn't stop his muscles from tightening.

He couldn't imagine why anyone would want to hurt Sadie.

And he couldn't imagine Sadie not telling the truth either.

However, if she had assumed a false identity, then what else was she hiding?

He'd given that jacket and hat to Larchmont. Maybe Trevor would receive an update soon.

Trevor had a lot of questions.

Like a storm popping up out of nowhere on a cloudless day, nothing was as it seemed.

Sadie's heart beat harder.

The request to hire this stranger had slipped from her lips before she could stop it.

Yet another part of her thought the idea made sense.

This man had saved her once. He'd proven at least some part of him was noble.

There was still so much Sadie didn't know about herself and about what had happened and why. As much as she'd like to think she could leave the hospital and resume normal life, she knew that wasn't possible—not in her current state, which may or may not change within the next few minutes, hours, days, months, or ever.

She prayed she had the money to cover whatever his expenses were.

Perhaps she could sell her SUV if she had to. She didn't know.

The doctor had already told her they'd keep her in the hospital for observation at least through the night. Then tomorrow hopefully some of her memories would return and she'd know more about herself. What her career was. If she had coworkers or family.

What did she do for a living?

She tried to guess but no ideas popped into her mind.

Nothing was certain right now, and everything felt off-kilter because of it.

Maybe the detective would have some answers for her soon.

Dr. Conroy came back into the room. Did a few things on the computer. Let out a grunt.

"What is it?" Bennett asked.

"I have no idea how those orders got into the system."

"Don't you have a way of tracking things?" Bennett shifted, still looking annoyed.

"We do. And according to this, I put in this order. But I didn't."

She didn't like the sound of that.

"Who else could have done it?" Bennett asked.

"That's what I need to figure out. No one has access to my badge or sign-in."

"If you didn't do it, then obviously, someone else does have access to those things," Trevor added.

Conroy turned away from the computer, his expression grim. "You're right. Kate, don't give our patient any medications without talking to me first. Do you understand?"

"Yes, sir."

Then the doctor turned to Detective Bennett. "I can ask one of our IT guys to figure out how this was done. But it's beyond me how this could have happened."

"I definitely want to talk to someone. Just give me a minute." Bennett turned back to Sadie, shifting as he stood beside her bed. "I'm going to continue looking into things. In the meantime, you get your rest. Heal. Maybe some memories will return. I'll check in tomorrow. But if anything comes up in the meantime, here's my card."

He placed it on the table beside her bed before

stepping from the room with Conroy, leaving just her and Trevor.

Sadie glanced at Trevor and saw him shift awkwardly. She couldn't blame him.

This was a strange situation for him to be in. He was an innocent bystander who'd been pulled into the sudden mess of her life. He probably had other plans. Now his day had been taken up with her, and the rest of his vacation had also been hijacked. Maybe she shouldn't have asked him to stay.

Yet she couldn't bring herself to withdraw the request either.

As he gazed at her, a strange rush of attraction swept through her.

Attraction? She had no right to feel attracted to this man. She didn't even know him.

She didn't even know *herself*.

She remembered that text on her phone. *Running a few minutes late. Can't wait to see you.*

It could have been to a boyfriend for all she knew. Though she wasn't wearing a ring, that didn't mean she wasn't married or in a serious relationship.

What if she had a husband? What if she had a child? Or two?

But then, why wouldn't she have any contacts in her phone and only one text?

Any attraction she felt to this Trevor man needed to be squashed immediately.

There were too many unknowns.

Just then, her phone rang on the table beside her.

She stared at it a minute, her pulse speeding.

Someone was calling her.

A loved one? A friend?

If so, why did she feel so much trepidation.

"Should I answer?" She glanced at Trevor.

"Definitely. Put it on speaker, if you don't mind. This could be someone with answers for you."

With shaky hands, she grabbed the phone.

The number on the screen didn't have a name attached to it—not that she'd expected it to.

She hit Talk and then Speaker. "Hello?"

Then she waited to hear who was on the other end.

CHAPTER
SEVEN

TREVOR WAITED for the caller to speak.

Only silence stretched across the line.

"Hello?" Sadie asked again.

Again, there was silence.

Trevor stepped closer, his muscles bristling as he asked, "Who is this?"

Nothing.

He glanced at the screen and saw the call had ended.

Whoever was on the other line didn't want to be known.

So why had they called? To see if she would answer? To find out if she'd survived?

Or maybe to put fear into her?

Coward.

Trevor glanced at Sadie and saw a tremble had overtaken her arms.

He swallowed hard, again resisting the urge to reach out and offer comfort.

It was even harder to keep his distance knowing how alone she was. She needed someone in her corner.

He had planned to be that person. It was too bad this situation was so complicated.

She might have been planted in his life by an enemy. He had to remember that.

"Who could that have been?" She looked up at him with wide eyes, imploring him for answers.

"I'm not sure. But I can try to find out for you."

"How?" She continued to stare at him. "I thought you were a bodyguard."

"I am. I'm also former military. Our security group not only provides protection to people, but we also do investigations. I'd be happy to see what I can find out if you'd like."

"Yes," she answered quickly. "Please. I'm desperate to know more."

"Anyone in your shoes would be. The tricky part is that I can't ask you any questions. I'll need to talk to people who know you—as soon as I can find out what you do for a living."

"Of course."

"If it's okay, I'd like to call in a colleague to help. That way one of us can keep an eye on you while the other does some research."

"Whatever you think is best," Sadie told him. "Even if I don't have money now, I promise I will pay you. I think I'm good for it. And if I'm not, I'll find a way to pay you back."

"I know you will." The words slipped out, and he swallowed hard.

Sadie clearly caught on to his choice of words because she tilted her head and raised an eyebrow.

"I mean, I just sense that you're a good person," he explained. "You seem like the type who wouldn't leave me hanging out to dry."

"I hope you're right. I hope I *am* a good person."

Trevor remembered again what Larchmont had told him. About how Sadie might not be who she claimed. How she could be using him.

Certainly, there was no truth to his boss's words.

Trevor would prove Larchmont was wrong if it was the last thing that he did.

The nurse came in to do a few procedures on Sadie, so Trevor slipped back into the hallway, promising to stay close.

As soon as he left the room, Sadie missed him.

Which was crazy considering she didn't know the man.

But maybe God had placed him in her life at just the right time and the right place.

And who knows but that you have come to your royal position for such a time as this?

Wait . . . was that a Bible verse?

She knew it was. Did that mean she was a believer?

She knew with this strange certainty that she was. She couldn't explain it. It was just something she sensed.

Were there other things she could sense also?

She pressed her eyes closed as the nurse took her vitals.

Maybe if Sadie lay still long enough and let her mind go another memory would emerge.

But as she lay there, trying not to move, nothing came.

Where memories should be, an empty void loomed.

Then a memory did hit her.

A recent one.

A memory of that phone call she'd just received.

What had that been about? Why hadn't the caller said something?

Nothing made sense.

Before she could think about it any longer, a commotion sounded in the hallway.

She sucked in a breath.

What was going on?

What if the person who'd tried to kill her earlier had come here . . . to finish what he or she started?

CHAPTER EIGHT

TREVOR SAW the man striding toward Sadie's room, clearly on a mission.

The man was built like a linebacker with dark hair and beefy arms. He wore khakis and a dark polo shirt, and his gaze was hooded.

Instantly, Trevor planted himself between the man and Sadie's hospital room, crossing his arms. "Who are you?"

The man glared at him. "Who are *you*?"

Trevor didn't answer. "The patient in this room isn't taking visitors right now."

"I think she'll make an exception for me." The guy grabbed Trevor's shoulder and tried to shove him out of the way.

The stranger had touched him. That was this guy's first mistake.

Trevor stiffened, refusing to move. "You don't want to do that."

The man's eyes narrowed. "I don't need you telling me what I do and do not want to do. Move."

He didn't budge.

The men stared off.

Then the door opened behind Trevor, and Nurse Kate peeked out at them, a wrinkle of concern between her eyes. "What's going on out here?"

The man peered around Trevor. "I'm here to see Sadie. This guy is trying to stop me."

"Who are you?" the nurse asked.

"My name is Guy Merchant. I'm Sadie's boyfriend."

Everything went still around Trevor.

Her boyfriend? Wait . . .

Trevor quickly hid his confusion.

But this guy had to be lying, right? Sadie hadn't had a boyfriend while she'd been dating Trevor. She wasn't the player type.

She was the type to bring food to the sick. To go out of her way to help someone in need. To stay inside for the weekend and read a book.

"My boyfriend?" Sadie asked from her hospital bed. She'd clearly seen the confrontation and heard part of the conversation between Trevor and Guy in the hallway.

Trevor stepped back, knowing he shouldn't stop

this guy anymore. It would only make more of a scene at this point.

The man walked into Sadie's room. Paused by her bed and took Sadie's hand into both of his as he stared at her.

"I'm so glad you're okay," the man murmured. "I was so worried."

Sadie stared at the man, no flash of recognition in her gaze. In fact, she almost looked frightened.

Trevor stepped into the room behind the man, knowing he had to get to the bottom of this—even if he didn't like the truth he discovered.

Sadie stared at the man standing beside her bed grasping her hand.

She wanted to recognize him. To feel something. To instinctively know she could trust him.

But she felt nothing.

She didn't remember ever seeing this man before.

"What's going on?" Sadie turned to Trevor.

"This guy tried to get into the room," Trevor said. "I tried to stop him. He didn't want to listen."

The nurse excused herself to take another call, leaving the three of them there to sort things out.

Sadie's gaze went back to the man holding her hand. "Who are you?"

"You mean, it's true?" Surprise raced through his gaze, and his grip on her hand loosened. "You really don't remember?"

"I'm sorry, but I don't."

He lowered his eyelids as if trying to cover a flinch. "I'm Guy Merchant. Your boyfriend for the past three months."

Her boyfriend? For three months? His name wasn't even vaguely familiar. Guy was a total stranger.

"How did you know to come here?" Trevor's voice held an edge of caution.

She was so glad Trevor had followed this guy into her room. She wanted Trevor here—especially until she knew who she could trust.

"A Detective Bennett came into the office and asked if anyone knew Sadie. When he told us you'd been in an accident and were here at the hospital, I told him I'd come out. He warned me you were having some memory issues."

Sadie supposed that explanation made sense.

She studied Guy, hoping for some flicker of recognition. There was still none. "If you're my boyfriend, what can you tell me about myself?"

He stared at her again, not bothering to hide his confusion. "You really don't remember anything?"

"I don't."

He let out a slow breath. "Your name is Sadie

Carrington. You are thirty-three years old. You're an only child, and you were raised in Florida, but you moved to Michigan for a job."

"A job where?"

"Sleeping Bear Elevator."

The name didn't ring any bells. "How did the two of us meet?"

"We work at the same company," Guy said. "We started having lunch together. I asked you to dinner. You said yes. And the rest, as they say, is history." Guy nodded toward the door. "I want to get you out of here. Maybe if I take you home you'll remember something."

Sadie flinched. The thought of leaving the hospital with this man terrified her.

The reaction didn't make sense. She didn't know Trevor either yet, for some reason, she trusted Trevor more.

She glanced at Trevor, helplessness wafting through her.

She didn't like feeling helpless. Not at all.

"I'm . . ." She looked back at Guy. "I'm going to need some time."

His eyes narrowed. "What do you mean?"

"I just mean . . . I'm not ready to make any big decisions. I need to think this through."

"So you don't want me to take you home?" A

touch of impatience tinged his voice. "I came all the way out here to see you."

"It's like I said . . . I need some time. And the doctor wants to keep me overnight."

Then Sadie waited to see if he'd continue to argue with her and grow more irritated—both of which would be sure signs she'd made the right decision.

CHAPTER
NINE

TREVOR'S MIND raced as he watched the interaction.

He didn't like any of this.

Had Sadie been cheating on Guy?

Had she been dating Guy for three months, and then started to see Trevor?

She hadn't struck him as a cheater.

Then again, nothing Larchmont had told him had struck Trevor as the truth.

But what if it was?

Or what if . . . this guy was a fake? After all, if someone was trying to kill Sadie, there was no better way to do so than by pretending to be someone she could trust.

Trevor sucked in a breath as he realized he was essentially doing the same thing. He was purposefully deceiving Sadie. Could he really live with himself for doing this?

Right now, he didn't have much choice.

The best thing he could do was to find answers—about her secrets, her identity.

He couldn't back out now. The stakes were too high.

He would have to let this play out.

Either way, he had some research to do.

Right now, Sadie gazed at him, her eyes pleading with him to help.

He stepped closer to Guy. "She asked you for some time."

Guy stepped back, his eyes narrowed. "I'm sorry, who are you? I don't think you ever said."

The question wasn't one of confusion or desperation. Instead, Guy barked the words as if he demanded an answer.

"He saved me," Sadie said before Trevor could respond. "Now I've hired him."

"Hired him?" Guy's voice rose. "A stranger?" Then Guy turned back to Trevor. "You are officially relieved of your duties. I'm here now, and I can take care of her. She's *my* girlfriend."

Trevor's jaw hardened. "You're not the one who hired me. I'll go when Sadie tells me to go."

Guy's eyes narrowed, and he let out a condescending chuckle. "Sadie isn't in her right mind. She doesn't know what she's saying or what she wants."

Trevor resisted the growl that wanted to emerge. This guy rubbed him the wrong way—on more than one level. "She knows enough to know she would like me to protect her."

"*I* should be the one protecting her." Guy pointed at himself, his eyes bulging.

"Enough!"

Both men turned toward Sadie. The confusion had slipped from her gaze, and in its place was white-hot irritation.

Maybe Trevor shouldn't have argued with Guy so much. After all, Sadie *did* have a head injury also. Their voices had risen right along with their testosterone. It couldn't be good for her recovery.

Trevor waited to hear what she had to say. Waited to see if he'd be fired.

If so, how would he stay close to her?

How would he find answers and keep her safe?

Sadie's head pounded.

Thankfully, both men had shut up. Now they stared at her, waiting for her to make a decision.

Only she didn't know what the right decision was. She only knew what she wanted.

And that was for Guy to leave.

Maybe the choice defied logic. Maybe it didn't make sense. Maybe she'd even regret it. She had no idea.

She swallowed hard and licked her lips before looking at Guy. "Do I have any pets?"

"What?"

"Do I need to send someone to take care of a dog or cat? I can't remember, so . . ."

Guy stared at her a moment before shaking his head. "No dogs or cats."

"Fish or birds?"

His gaze narrowed. "No."

"What about my parents? Should I call them? Will they be worried?"

He hesitated again before saying, "They passed away when you were young."

Sadie stared at him another moment before shrugging and letting out a sigh. "I don't know what to say. I just need some time. I'm not ready to make any big decisions or leave."

"So you want to stay here with this stranger?" Guy pointed his thumb toward Trevor as if the man were a lunatic.

"He's here because I asked him to be here not because he insisted on it. Besides, right now, everyone is a stranger."

Guy threw his hands up. "What if he can't be trusted?"

"I'm sorry, but right now I don't know if I can trust you either." She swallowed hard again as she saw the hurt wash through Guy's gaze.

He ran a hand over his face. "Don't do this, Sadie."

"I'm sorry. I truly do need time. I'm so . . . overwhelmed. I know you want to help me navigate this, but I'm not ready yet."

Guy slowly nodded before taking a reluctant step back. "You and all your boundaries . . . I guess I shouldn't be surprised."

With one last scathing glare at Trevor, Guy stepped out of the room and shut the door behind him.

Then Sadie turned to Trevor as he stood on the other side of her bed. His entire body appeared taut and defensive, as if he'd been ready to pounce on Guy if it had become necessary.

Guy's protectiveness had bothered her. Trevor's did not.

Why was that?

"Did I do the right thing?" A touch of doubt filled her voice.

"Guy needs to respect your boundaries. If what you need is for him not to pressure you right now, then you absolutely did the right thing."

Trevor's words filled her with a surprising measure of comfort and reassurance.

Having someone here who understood her did wonders for her mental well-being.

But she still had so much she needed to figure out.

"Trevor . . . I saw a man out the window." She rubbed her throat. "I don't know why, but he made me uneasy."

Trevor's muscles tightened. "When?"

"Maybe thirty or forty minutes ago. I don't know where he went."

"Can you describe him?"

She shook her head. "He was wearing all black."

"You didn't recognize him?"

She licked her lips. "No, it was just a feeling."

A strange emotion crossed Trevor's face. But as quickly as it appeared, it was gone.

Did he know something she didn't?

Or was her mind just playing tricks on her?

CHAPTER
TEN

AN HOUR LATER, Trevor's backup arrived, and Larchmont disappeared.

Kai Kaleo, part California boy and part Polynesian. He and Trevor had worked together for the past few years, and Trevor knew he could depend on him.

Sadie needed to rest. The best way to heal from some of the trauma her body had been through was by getting some sleep.

He told Sadie goodbye, and then he gave Kai the rundown on the situation. Then, knowing Sadie was in good hands, he headed out.

He needed to do his own research and find some answers.

He left the hospital, glancing at everything as he passed. He halfway expected trouble to be lurking in the shadows.

But he didn't see anything that raised any alarms.

He climbed into his truck, made a couple of phone calls, and then typed an address into his GPS.

Trevor had already looked up Guy Merchant on his phone. He knew where the man lived. If no one was home, Trevor planned on sneaking inside. If Guy was home, Trevor planned on watching him.

He *would* find some answers.

He headed down the street, making several turns. Fifteen minutes later, he spotted Guy's house. It was a dark red-brick ranch home with a neatly kept yard and decent-sized lot.

He parked down the road, far enough away not to be seen, but close enough to keep an eye on the place.

He'd already had Larchmont look into Guy, but nothing suspicious had turned up.

The man really did work at the elevator company. He was thirty-five. Divorced. No children.

But something about him gave Trevor a bad feeling.

Could that reaction be born of jealousy? Maybe.

When Trevor had met Sadie, she'd told him she hadn't dated in three years, not since she and her fiancé had broken up. She'd seemed so sincere as she'd told him about that prior relationship and how she'd needed time to recover.

So what was all this "boyfriend" business about?

Nothing made sense.

Trevor settled back in his seat and stared at Guy's Mercedes in the driveway.

The man must have taken the rest of the day off work, and Trevor planned on staying here for as long as necessary to watch for anything suspicious.

An hour later, Guy stepped out the front door, glanced around, and then hurried to his car.

Trevor waited until the man had pulled out of the driveway before putting his truck in Drive and pulling out behind him. He kept a safe distance behind the man, curious to see where he was headed.

They wove through the streets of Traverse City, toward the downtown area.

A few minutes later, Guy pulled into the parking lot of a local Italian restaurant.

This could make things more complicated. But this could also be Trevor's chance to find out more information.

He pulled onto the side of the road and waited. Then he saw Guy walk toward the front door and meet another man there.

Trevor snapped a picture. Maybe he could identify this guy.

Then he slipped inside the restaurant.

Before the hostess could address him, he peered across the dining area and saw Guy seated at a booth. Beside the table was a wooden partition that stretched only halfway to the ceiling.

If Trevor could get a seat on the other side, maybe he could hear what these guys were talking about. Thankfully, this place wasn't too busy.

"Can I help you?" the hostess asked. "Just one?"

Trevor kept his head low so Guy wouldn't spot him. "I was wondering if I might get a booth. Maybe over there out of the flow of traffic?"

"Sure, we have some booths open in that section." She grabbed a laminated menu.

"Perfect."

Still keeping his head low, Trevor walked toward the booth. The scent of garlic and pasta filled the air, making his stomach grumble. He was hungrier than he'd thought.

He slipped into the seat on the same side as Guy. He had a better chance of not being spotted here. Thankfully, the partition was high enough that Guy shouldn't see him either.

As the waitress handed him a menu, Trevor forced a smile and tried to look casual. But instead of studying tonight's specials, his ear tuned to the conversation beside him.

It was just some local sports talk right now.

Which seemed like an interesting choice considering that Guy's supposed girlfriend had almost been killed.

He tuned them out a moment and ordered some spaghetti and garlic bread.

As he closed the menu, he glanced around at the other patrons in the restaurant. No one suspicious caught his eye.

Then he spotted a police officer walking toward him.

Trevor's muscles tensed. Was the man coming to arrest him? To bring him to the station?

Instead, the officer continued past and slid into the booth behind him.

Trevor released his breath.

Trevor had seen a twentysomething woman sitting there.

"Hey," the woman said. "You're late."

"I was working on a case."

Trevor wondered if this guy was referring to Sadie's case.

Then the man said, "You'll never believe this. But we found a dead body in the woods not far from the sand dunes."

Trevor's lungs froze.

A dead body?

He remembered the blood he'd found on Sadie's arm and hands.

But he refused to think those two things were

connected.

Sadie wasn't a killer, and no one could convince him otherwise.

CHAPTER
ELEVEN

EVERYTHING WENT STILL around Trevor as he listened. He needed to know more.

"Who is it?" the woman asked.

"I don't know," the officer said. "We haven't identified him yet."

"So he's not a local?"

"Doesn't appear to be. But this guy probably was killed sometime early this morning."

This morning? Trevor mused. That would have been about the time he'd found Sadie.

What if Larchmont was right? What if Sadie wasn't really her name? What if she had some type of secret life he wasn't privy to?

Trevor couldn't imagine what that life might be. But it wouldn't be wise of him to ignore the possibility. He'd worked many classified missions. It stood to reason that some of the enemies he'd made might want to find him. Might want to know what he knew.

Did Sadie have anything to do with that dead body?

Trevor didn't want to believe it could be true. But he needed to face reality and examine it as a possibility.

He texted the update to Larchmont.

Trevor needed to stay here now and find out what Guy knew. But Larchmont could send someone else to look into this dead man.

"Why do you think he was murdered?" the woman behind him asked.

"You know all the drug problems we've been having in this area lately," the officer said. "My guess is that it had something to do with that. Maybe a drug deal gone bad? It's hard to say right now."

"I hate hearing that. I wish I could scrub all those things from this area."

"You and me both," the officer said. "Anyway, enough about work. How was your day?"

The conversation between the two shifted to soccer and an upcoming concert.

Instead, Trevor turned his attention to Guy on the other side of the partition instead.

But Guy and his friend continued to chat about inconsequential things.

Which still seemed strange.

Why wouldn't Guy be more concerned about his girlfriend?

Trevor waited patiently, hoping the conversation would change.

In the meantime, Trevor scanned the restaurant. Several people had come in and were talking about the dead body.

Word traveled fast in smaller towns like this.

His food was delivered, and he slowly ate, taking his time so he wouldn't miss anything. On the plus side, the spaghetti was delicious.

Then the conversation beside him shifted.

Guy lowered his voice as he said, "I don't know what's going on, and I don't know what you want me to do about it."

"You need to handle it."

"You're acting like I knew this would happen," Guy said.

"You should have seen it coming."

"Don't worry about it. I'll handle things."

Trevor's shoulders tightened.

Was he talking about Sadie? On one hand, Trevor could see where this might be a conversation with someone at work. That this could be innocent, and the emotions could simply be present because of the hit-and-run.

But the other part of Trevor wondered if there was something sinister behind the man's words.

Before he could listen anymore, he glanced at the window and saw a man peering inside.

Peering at him.

It was a different man than the one Trevor had chased at the hospital—the one who'd taken off after he'd been spotted.

When he saw Trevor had noticed him, the man darted away.

Trevor dropped some money on the table and then took off.

He didn't want to make a scene, but this guy couldn't get away either.

Just as he sprinted outside, the man ran toward the woods.

Where was this guy going?

The man turned around.

Trevor saw something in his hands.

A gun.

The next instant, gunfire exploded through the air.

Trevor ducked behind a car. People around him screamed and ducked for cover

He peered up to check the situation.

Saw the man had taken off again.

Trevor dashed after him.

But as they ran, the man continued to fire.

Was this guy trying to kill him?

Sirens were already sounding. No doubt the officer in the restaurant had called for backup.

Trevor might take out his own gun. But only as a last resort.

The man ducked behind a thrift store in the distance.

Trevor cut through a small patch of trees, trying to reach him in time.

But just as Trevor emerged from the tree line, a car pulled up to the curb.

The man jumped inside.

As the car pulled away, he glanced back at Trevor once more.

His face was concealed by his hat, making his features impossible to distinguish.

Trevor wouldn't let that stop him.

He was determined to figure out what was going on here.

CHAPTER
TWELVE

BY THE TIME Trevor got back to the sidewalk, the officer who'd been seated behind him in the restaurant caught up. Officer Blanche, his name badge read.

"What's going on?" Blanche demanded.

Trevor raised his hands to show he wasn't the shooter. "I saw a man watching me and went outside to see why. He opened fire on me."

The officer narrowed his eyes as if he didn't believe him. "Who are you?"

"Trevor McGrath."

"You ever see that guy before?"

"No, I haven't. But I've been hired as a bodyguard for Sadie Carrington, the woman who was hit by a car earlier today at the beach."

Realization captured Blanche's face. "I see. You're

going to need to wait here. I'll have more questions for you."

"Of course."

He pulled a pad of paper from his pocket. "Did you see the guy's car? The license plate?"

Trevor shared the information, and the officer put his radio to his mouth and recited it to his coworkers, who were probably already in their patrol cars trying to find the shooter.

Trevor glanced around. It appeared no one had been hurt.

At least that was something to be thankful for.

Before Officer Blanche could question him any longer, a new figure stalked toward him.

Guy Merchant.

And the man didn't look happy.

"What are you doing here?" Guy demanded, pausing in front of Trevor. The veins bulged at his temples, and his breathing looked shallow.

Trevor made sure not to react but to remain placid instead. "Maybe the better question is, what are *you* doing here?"

Guy scowled. "Are you following me? Spying on me?"

"Please, don't flatter yourself," Trevor said. "I was

having dinner—not that I need to explain that to you."

"Well, *somebody* needs to start explaining *something*." The man's chest puffed up with entitlement.

Officer Blanche turned to Guy. "Back off. We have other things to worry about rather than your ego right now."

Trevor tried not to smirk at the man's words, but it was difficult.

Guy scowled and crossed his arms, but he didn't say anything else.

However, he patiently waited as the officer questioned Trevor.

Trevor told Blanche everything he knew, which wasn't much. Well, maybe he didn't tell him *everything*. But he told the officer about the situation that had happened both earlier and now here at the restaurant.

Then the officer looked back and forth between Trevor and Guy.

"So you're acting as security for Ms. Carrington," he glanced at Trevor then Guy, "and you're her boyfriend?"

Guy's scowl deepened. "She has amnesia, so everything is kind of upside down right now."

"You can't even write this stuff." The officer jotted something down before shaking his head.

Trevor could agree with him on that.

But the truth was, Trevor had questions for Guy. Questions Guy no doubt wouldn't want to answer.

Trevor decided to ask them anyway.

He locked his gaze on Guy's, not bothering to hide the challenge in his eyes. "You looked awfully relaxed back there for someone whose girlfriend was nearly killed in a hit-and-run."

His nostrils flared. "That's none of your business. I just needed to blow off some steam."

"I'm no expert on human behavior, but that didn't look like blowing off steam. That looked more like apathy."

Guy's hands fisted at his sides.

The man clearly had a temper.

Even if Sadie had lied to Trevor . . . Even if she had been dating someone else . . . Even if she wasn't who she said she was . . . Trevor prayed she wasn't involved with Guy.

The man was a total hothead.

Trevor couldn't help but wonder if Guy had something to do with what had happened today . . . either concerning Sadie or the dead man found in the woods.

CHAPTER
THIRTEEN

THE NEXT MORNING, the nurse helped Sadie get dressed. She'd been given some clothing from the donation bin at the hospital—black sweats, a pale pink T-shirt, and flip-flops one size too large.

Her whole body was sore today, and it hurt to move. But what bugged her most was the fact her memory still hadn't returned.

She'd naively hoped she'd go to sleep, wake up, and everything would be back to normal. Everything would make sense.

Instead, *nothing* had made sense. In fact, she felt more confused than ever.

She'd had a dream, however. At least, she thought it was a dream. Maybe she hoped it was a memory.

In the sequence, she'd been on the beach laughing with someone. The beautiful waters of

Lake Michigan had been sparkling in front of her. A breeze had rushed through her hair. Sand speckled her skin.

Then she'd stood and grabbed someone's hand. They'd run toward the water.

But she'd hadn't just grabbed *anyone's* hand.

She'd grabbed the hand of a man.

Someone Sadie was nearly certain she was in love with.

But every time she looked up and tried to see his face, she couldn't make out any details. Everything was blurry.

In the dream, that hadn't mattered. All that had mattered was the overwhelming happiness she felt.

As the two of them had reached the water, the man had scooped her into his arms as he waded deeper.

She'd squealed and told him he better not throw her in.

Bliss had captured her—bliss that left a horrible ache when she'd awoken and realized it wasn't real.

Or was it?

Who was the mystery man with her? Guy?

Could what he'd told her be true? Were the two of them really dating and in love?

Sadie didn't know. But she needed to talk to some of her coworkers or neighbors or friends so she could figure out exactly what the truth was.

Certainly, someone would know if she was dating.

Then there was one other thing, she mused as the nurse finished helping her and left.

Somewhere in the middle of that dream/memory, her stomach had tightened.

Tell him your secret.

The words had wafted through her mind.

Her secret? She didn't know what it was.

She only knew at the core of her being that it would change everything.

Then she'd seen a man in the distance. He'd had a knife. As he lunged toward her, she'd screamed, and her dream had ended.

Nothing made sense, and the realization almost made her want to give up.

Was she a quitter? She didn't think so.

But she felt so alone that her heart physically ached.

Maybe she should call Guy. Ask him more questions. Ask him to take her to all the places where she might remember something.

Yet something internal stopped her from doing that.

It didn't make sense. She didn't know what her mental block might be.

But she couldn't deny that feelings of caution were there.

She needed to trust her gut.

A knock sounded at the door, and her breath caught.

She looked over, hoping it might be Trevor.

She knew he'd left one of his colleagues outside her room all night. In fact, the man had poked his head into the room to check on her several times.

Instead of Trevor, however, it was Detective Bennett.

Sadie tried to hide her disappointment. Then she realized he might have an update for her, and she perked up. He'd sent an officer last night to take her fingerprints, and she was anxious to hear if he'd discovered anything.

He took a chair across from her, and the nurse scurried from the room to give them privacy. This was a different nurse from yesterday, and she seemed much more skittish than Kate.

"Any changes this morning?" He sat upright, his voice professional but concerned.

Sadie remembered that dream again but knew she couldn't mention it. Mostly because the dream didn't mean anything concrete. There was no certainty in any of it. People had dreams all the time that didn't match reality.

"No, unfortunately there haven't been changes." Sadie tried to conceal the disappointment in her voice.

Bennett pressed his lips together grimly and nodded. "I see."

"Have you found out anything? Did you find the person who did this?"

"We ran the plates that Mr. McGrath gave us."

"And?" She held her breath as she waited for him to continue.

"His recollection of the plates was correct. That vehicle did in fact hit you. We found damage on it."

Her breath caught, and a moment of hope filled her chest. As quickly as the feeling appeared, it began to shrivel as the detective's tone echoed in her head. "Why do I feel like there's a but in there?"

Bennett frowned. "Unfortunately, the vehicle was stolen, and there were no viable prints. So we don't have any leads on who may have been behind the wheel. They abandoned it on the outskirts of town."

"Did any cameras nearby pick up on who may have been driving it?" she asked.

Amnesia was a strange thing. Sadie couldn't remember her past, yet she could remember that cameras were located on streets in the downtown area? It was all so very peculiar and didn't make sense.

"We're still checking, hoping to figure something out, but so far there's nothing."

"I assume you've confirmed that my name truly is Sadie Carrington? That I really am thirty-three years old, and that I work for . . . who do I work for again?"

"Your fingerprints check out. We confirmed that you work for Sleeping Bear Elevator Company."

Her jaw tightened. That meant that what Guy said was true.

The detective handed her a paper bag he'd brought into the room with him. "These are some items we recovered from your vehicle. Your purse, which contains a few personal effects as well as credit cards and some cash."

"Did you search the rest of my car and find anything?"

"We checked it out, but we didn't find anything of note," Detective Bennett said. "Just what was to be expected. Nothing that gave us any indication as to who might have done this to you, however."

Sadie tried to hide her disappointment and keep some semblance of hope alive. They were just beginning the investigation. They still had time to discover more information.

"Did you talk to my coworkers?" she asked. "Maybe one of them has an idea of who might want to hurt me. Although, I don't really know how competitive my job would be at an elevator company."

"We're in the middle of talking to everyone there

now. But so far, your coworkers are as shocked as you are. I assure you we'll keep looking into this."

Sadie frowned but nodded.

She'd been hoping for something more concrete. But in reality, she didn't know any more right now than she did before the detective had come into her room.

Trevor headed from the elevator to Sadie's room.

He'd intended on coming back last night, but too much had happened.

After he'd left the restaurant, he'd gone to Sadie's Bronco in the parking lot. The police hadn't towed it yet.

He searched through it, but he'd found nothing.

Then he'd picked the lock at her house, snuck inside, and looked around for anything that might give him a clue about what was going on.

Again, he'd found nothing.

Strangely nothing.

This was his first time inside her place. She had a rule about bringing guys here, she'd told him.

But he was still surprised.

Sadie had very few personal effects inside. A couple of pictures of her by herself, one at the Grand

Canyon and another at what appeared to be a Florida beach.

There were no photo albums or files that gave him any insight—no birth certificate, tax returns, or warranty information even.

It was almost like she'd made a clean start when she moved into the place.

Sadie, however, seemed like the type who would like mementos of the places she'd been or lived. Who would put up pictures of loved ones and friends. Who would have cozy blankets and cookie-scented candles.

By the time he'd done all that, it was late. Trevor had gone back to his hotel to get some shuteye while Kai kept an eye on things. Then he'd awakened bright and early to come back to the hospital. Before leaving, he'd packed his overnight bag.

He'd move to a new hotel tonight, just to be on the safe side.

Kai nodded from outside Sadie's hospital room as Trevor approached.

"Any updates?" Trevor paused in front of him.

"The detective is in there with her now. No other visitors or anything suspicious."

That was good news. But Trevor didn't feel any better. Danger and unanswered questions still seemed to close in from every side.

"What's this about a dead body that was found

outside town?" Kai narrowed his eyes in concern. "Any updates?"

Larchmont had called Trevor with an update this morning.

The man who died was John Breckenridge. He was thirty-eight. From Wisconsin. Supposedly in town to kayak.

He'd been killed via knife wound to the gut.

That was all they knew so far. Both the police and Larchmont were continuing to dig.

His boss had sent a picture of John. The man had thick brown hair, darker skin, and a small build.

Larchmont also said they found a hair on the hat abandoned by the man who'd fled from the hospital. They were running it through the system for DNA, but so far hadn't had any hits.

Also, the man Guy had met with at the restaurant last night had been a friend from high school, a man without any criminal record. The dinner could have truly been casual. But Trevor was reserving his judgment.

Trevor shared what he knew with Kai.

Kai stepped closer and lowered his voice. "I overheard the nurse and doctor talking this morning. They indicated Sadie would probably be cleared to go home soon."

"I figured as much. That's why I've been trying to get everything lined up so I can take her there. Did they say anything about the medication mix-up yesterday?"

"Only that they were still trying to figure out what happened," Kai said. "Did you check out her house?"

"I did." Trevor nodded. "I didn't find anything useful."

"How about her SUV? Did you have a chance to look in it?"

"I did. But again, there was nothing. It's all strange. I'm not done with this yet, however. Something's not adding up."

Kai's jaw twitched. "What do you need me to do?"

"You've been working all night. You go get some rest, and I'll take over for now. I'll give you a call later."

"Understood." With a nod, Kai headed down the hallway, relieved of his duties.

Only a few seconds later, the door to Sadie's hospital room opened, and Detective Bennett stepped out. His eyes widened with recognition and surprise when he saw Trevor standing there.

Trevor wasn't sure if the detective trusted him or not. The man definitely seemed cautious, but Trevor couldn't blame him. Any good detective would be.

"Good morning, Mr. McGrath." The detective nodded.

"Morning." Trevor's gaze traveled behind him, and he saw Sadie sitting in a chair. Her hair had been washed and combed, and she wore fresh but ill-fitting clothes.

"I assume you're still keeping an eye on Ms. Carrington."

"That's right," Trevor said. "At least until she regains some of her memories or you guys apprehend whoever tried to kill her."

Something darkened in the detective's gaze, but the shadow had only been a flicker. It disappeared as quickly as it had materialized. "I assure you that we're working on it."

"I'm glad to hear that." Trevor had to be careful. If the detective dug too deeply, he might find out things about Trevor that needed to remain buried.

The agency was good at what they did. Good at covering their tracks. But there was always the possibility that some small detail would fall through the cracks—a small detail that could lead to major consequences.

Even though they'd been hired by the government for multiple assignments, the government would claim ignorance if they were ever pressed. They wouldn't come to his rescue or defense.

Trevor and his colleagues would be on their own.

Trevor needed to keep that in the back of his mind.

Always have a backup plan. Rule number one for covert op assignments. He knew that better than anyone.

As the detective walked away, Trevor took another step toward Sadie's room and knocked on the open door.

Sadie spotted him and nodded, giving him permission to come inside.

His throat went desert-dry as he got a better glimpse of her. Even after everything that had happened, she still looked gorgeous. Even in her sweats and oversized T-shirt. Even with her normally styled hair looking wavy with untamed strands and no makeup on her face.

The only difference was that she now looked gorgeous, secretive, *and* confused.

How had this turned into such a nightmare? Just yesterday morning, Trevor had been picturing himself spending the rest of his life with this woman.

The thought had been crazy, and he'd known that. They'd only been on four dates.

But there had been something special about Sadie.

Had the chemistry between them been an act?

Trevor didn't want to believe it.

"The doctor should have my discharge papers signed soon." Sadie offered a faint smile that didn't reach her eyes. "I'm ready to get out of here. And good news—they brought me my wallet, and I *do* have at least a little cash with me."

She was so worried about paying him what she'd promised. That sounded like Sadie. She wasn't the type to take advantage of anyone. At the store once, the cashier had given her an extra five-dollar bill. She'd gone back to return it.

"Like I said, don't worry about that right now," Trevor told her. "We'll get it all figured out later."

She studied him another moment. "If you're sure . . ."

"Of course." Trevor forced himself not to react to her gaze on him. He feared she might read too much into his expression. Might know there was more to the relationship than he was letting on.

Just then, his phone buzzed. It was Larchmont.

Trevor quickly glanced at the message.

> One last update I failed to mention earlier. We sent one of our guys to Sadie's office last night. He found a hidden cell phone taped beneath her desk. Still trying to unlock it. She's definitely hiding something.

CHAPTER
FOURTEEN

TWO HOURS LATER, Sadie stepped outside the hospital and drew in a deep breath.

Even though she'd only been in the building for less than twenty-four hours, the fresh air felt good—felt healing.

Trevor remained close to her, his hand near her elbow as if he feared she might topple over.

Although it wasn't necessary, she appreciated his concern and attention. The truth was, she didn't feel totally steady on her feet. Her head still had a slight throb, and the medications she'd been given left her feeling weak.

He ushered her to his truck, an older blue Chevy from the nineties that looked well taken care of.

Once she was tucked inside, Trevor jogged to the

driver's side and climbed in, slamming his door behind him.

He cranked the engine before turning to her. "I'm assuming you want to go home?"

She shivered as she realized she couldn't even remember what home looked like. "Yes, please. I'm hoping that something there—something familiar—will dredge up some memories."

"Nothing yet?"

She sucked on her bottom lip before shaking her head.

The dream she'd had last night flashed back into her mind. But she still wasn't sure if she could trust it. Who had that man been? A figment of her imagination? Or a real person in her life?

"Not really," she finally said. "The doctor has no idea when my memories will return. He said there's a possibility they *won't* return."

"That has to be a tough pill to swallow."

"For sure. Dr. Evans, the hospital psychologist, came in this morning. There's some therapy that might help, but she wants to see if I regain anything on my own first. I scheduled an appointment with her next week, as well as a follow-up with Dr. Conroy later this week."

"Let's hope you remember everything before then."

"Wouldn't that be nice?" She stared at the traffic

whizzing by on the street beside them and frowned. "I wonder where my Bronco is . . ."

"I heard the detective say he would have one of his guys bring it to your house."

"That's good news, I suppose. I would give you directions to my house but . . ." Her voice trailed in a weak attempt at humor.

"I'll just plug the address into my GPS if you don't mind reading it to me from your license."

She did that, and then they took off.

Sadie watched as Trevor's gaze scanned everything around them as they drove.

Just what she would expect from a bodyguard, she supposed. At the very least, the action made her feel safer.

Her thoughts continued to wander through what she did know. They wouldn't stop, and Sadie wasn't sure she wanted them to. But Dr. Conroy had warned her not to put too much mental stress on herself.

"I hope everyone is wrong," Sadie murmured after a few minutes of silence. "I hope that maybe the person who did this to me was just some crazy druggie who didn't realize what he was doing. I just can't imagine why someone would want to kill me."

"Someone driving under the influence of drugs or alcohol—or both—is a definite possibility," Trevor said.

She stared out the window, still waiting to recognize something and have some kind of ah-ha moment.

But she didn't.

As despair tried to bite deeply, she turned to Trevor, desperate for a distraction. "Tell me more about yourself."

He flinched as if surprised, but the reaction quickly faded as if he'd stowed it away, locked it up, and thrown away the key.

He shrugged. "Not much interesting to say about me."

"There must be. You're a bodyguard with experience in the military. You must like the beach since you were headed there yesterday when you found me. My understanding is that no one else was there. Were you just going to enjoy the view? Or do you do some type of water sports?"

"I was just headed to the beach to relax," Trevor said. "I'm thirty-four years old and originally from North Dakota. I joined the military right out of high school, really as soon as I could."

"Is that because you wanted to serve your country or because you had no idea what else you wanted to do?"

"Maybe a little of both. It seemed noble." He paused before continuing. "My mom was a single mom for years until she got remarried to a man who wanted nothing to do with me. He didn't tell my mom that, but he made it clear to me. One day, he pulled me aside and told me that as soon as I graduated I had to get out of the house, that he wasn't going to pay for a freeloader."

"That's terrible." A frown tugged at her lips at the thought.

Trevor nodded. "Leaving home right away wasn't my original plan, that's for sure. But my mom seemed so happy. I didn't want to break it to her that she'd married a jerk. I couldn't afford college on my own, so the military seemed like a good option."

"Is your mom still with this guy?"

"No. She eventually figured out for herself what kind of man he was. They divorced a couple of years later. My mom didn't handle it well. She overdosed on some pain meds and . . ." His voice cracked.

Sadie reached for his arm and squeezed it. "I'm so sorry. I shouldn't have asked."

"It's okay. There's no need to hide the truth, even when it's painful. I miss her every day, but time marches on, right?"

"It does, whether we want it to or not." She paused. "And now you work for a security agency that does jobs all over the US, but you just happen to be in Michigan right now taking a few days for vacation? And you showed up at the same secluded beach as me at just the right time?"

"There's more to it than that."

She stiffened. "What do you mean?"

"This was one of my mom's favorite places to vacation," Trevor told her. "So every year around her birthday, I try to come here and have some time of self-reflection. It makes me feel closer to her somehow."

"That's really beautiful."

It truly was. Sadie was enjoying—if *enjoying* was the right word—finding out more about Trevor. At least it was something concrete. It was better than thinking about the uncertainties of her own life.

"I think the shores of Lake Michigan are gorgeous," Trevor said. "Being on the water seems to make everything better, you know?"

A smile tugged at her lips. "Yeah, surprisingly, I do know. Even though I can't remember much, for some reason I know I love the beach."

Trevor cast a quick but faint smile her way. "It's a good place to love."

Before they could talk more, he stopped in front of a small bungalow located in an older, more established neighborhood full of similar homes.

This must be her house.

The place was so unfamiliar, however, that it almost felt eerie to be here.

Sadie braced herself for whatever she might find inside.

Trevor pushed down the grief simmering inside him. Even though he knew it was crazy to feel heartache over a relationship that had only been four dates deep, the feelings were still there.

Listening to Sadie talk had done all kinds of strange things to his heart.

She'd *loved* the beach. She'd adored it, actually.

He'd loved watching her stare at the water and soak in the sun and laugh as the waves hit her.

Now, all that could be gone. Those days might not ever be recreated. The possibility of their relationship might have died right along with her memories.

His gut clenched.

Maybe it was better this way.

Especially considering that hidden cell phone one of his colleagues had found in Sadie's office.

Why would she have a hidden cell phone? Why did she have blood on her hands? And what about that list of numbers she had in her beach bag?

He'd examined the list last night, but he still didn't know what the figures meant. He would keep searching.

He shoved those thoughts aside for now.

He hadn't told the truth earlier about his mom either. The truth was, he'd been on assignment in this area about a year ago taking down a human-trafficking ring. While here, he'd fallen in love with Michigan's beaches, and now he tried to come up here as often as he could.

Trevor ran around to Sadie's door and opened it for her, helping her out.

He knew she wasn't fragile, but he wanted to make sure she didn't have any more falls.

Head injuries were serious matters, and she didn't look steady on her feet yet.

"Do you have your keys?" He had picked the lock to get into her place last night, and he could do it again if needed. But he couldn't let her know that.

She reached into the paper bag they'd given her at the hospital and pulled out a set. "I'm assuming one of these will fit."

Trevor took them from her and walked beside her toward the door, which had been painted a cheerful yellow that fit her normally sunny demeanor.

When he reached the porch, his muscles went taut.

The door wasn't latched.

He knew without a doubt he'd closed this door last night after he finished inside. He'd been careful not to leave any sign he'd been there.

"Trevor?" Sadie's voice trembled as she watched his reaction.

"I need you to stay here." He handed the keys back to her, stealing a glance at her expression.

She'd gone pale.

Right now, however, his main concern was keeping her safe.

He pulled out his gun and carefully nudged the door open.

His eyes widened at what he saw.

The whole place had been ransacked and looked like someone had either been looking for something or trying to send a message. If they'd been trying to send a message, it had worked. Sadie was clearly shaken—as she should be.

He quickly glanced at Sadie again. "You should wait in the truck."

She shook her head. "If no one is here now then I want to see."

Trevor's gut tightened. He wasn't sure that was a good idea. But he knew by the look in her eyes that she wouldn't back down.

He gave her a nod before stepping inside. He quickly dodged the overturned furniture, scattered books, and ripped cushions on the floor as he searched the house for any intruders.

Just as he suspected, whoever had done this was now long gone. He shoved his gun back into his holster as he approached Sadie outside.

"It's clear." He led her into the living room and shut the door behind them, just to be on the safe side.

Her face paled as she glanced around the room and shook her head. "I can't believe this."

Neither could he.

"Should I call the police?" she asked.

"I'll do it for you." He pulled out his phone—his regular one that had no record of calls between him and Sadie—and made the call to Detective Bennett.

The detective promised to be right out and asked them not to touch anything.

Instead, he and Sadie stood in the doorway as they waited.

"Anything bringing back memories?" Trevor glanced at Sadie.

She shook her head, grim lines around her mouth and eyes. "No, nothing. Right now, it's even hard to believe I called this place home. It just looks like something that belongs to a stranger . . . and like a wreck."

"After the detective clears it, I'll help you get the place cleaned up."

She shivered as she continued staring at her living room. "Except I'm not sure I want to stay here. I'm wondering if a hotel might be a better option."

Trevor had the exact same thought. There were too many opportunities for someone to breach this place. A hotel room would be safer.

"I can arrange that," he said. "I'll use my credit card. We don't want someone tracing yours." Before Sadie could insist that she would pay him for any expenses, he jumped in with, "We'll make everything right when this is over."

Sadie studied him another moment and then nodded and looked away.

Trevor's gaze lingered on her as she stared at the mess in front of her.

He remembered back to only four nights ago when the two of them had been in front of each other.

They'd had dinner together. Then they'd gone to the beach. He'd walked her to her car and paused there.

They had been laughing, the chemistry between them easy and natural.

Then he'd leaned toward her and planted a long, slow kiss on her lips. She'd returned the kiss, and the two of them had become lost in the moment.

He'd been dreaming about that kiss ever since. Wanting to recreate it.

Now here they were alone again.

But no matter how much Trevor wanted to kiss her again, he couldn't. Not without her not knowing their past. Not until they discovered the truth about her past.

Maybe not even until Trevor could tell her the truth about his own life.

Before Trevor could think about it any longer, a police car pulled up outside.

He'd have to wallow in the remorse of those lost kisses later.

Right now, he had to focus on whoever was trying to kill Sadie.

CHAPTER
FIFTEEN

DETECTIVE BENNETT CAME AND WENT.

He'd checked out Sadie's place. Since Sadie didn't know if anything was missing, it made the investigation more difficult. But she couldn't, and she was tired of beating herself up for something she had no control over.

The detective had agreed it was a good idea to stay somewhere else. The person who'd hit her in the parking lot yesterday most likely knew where she lived.

In fact, this person seemed to know entirely too much about her.

The fact her place had been ransacked most likely meant the accident couldn't have been random.

It had been planned.

Someone had followed her to the beach. Or . . . someone had already known she would be there.

Sadie shivered at the thought.

She didn't have many answers, but she knew without a doubt this was far from over.

"I just want to grab a few things and change into some more presentable clothes." She looked down at her sweats and T-shirt before glancing back up at him. "Then I'd like to go to my office."

He squinted. "Are you sure you're up for that? Maybe resting would be a better idea."

"Maybe. But this can't wait. The sooner I find answers, the sooner I can put this whole nightmare behind me."

Trevor stared at her another moment, unreadable thoughts swirling behind his gaze. Finally, he said, "If that's what you want."

It was *definitely* what she wanted.

He walked beside her as she headed toward her bedroom. She only knew it was her bedroom because she'd walked around the house earlier, and this was the room with all her personal effects.

She found clothes to change into—some jeans and a teal top that was comfortable but fitted. She ran a brush through her hair and put on some makeup. Then she tracked down a bag in the closet and stuffed clothes and toiletries inside—anything she might need.

She started to hike the bag over her shoulder when Trevor took it from her. "I can carry this."

Sadie flushed, though she didn't know why. Had she not been around many gentlemen before?

It was impossible to say.

"Thank you," she murmured instead.

As Trevor led her back outside, she turned to take one more look at her house.

Part of her wanted to start cleaning right now, to try to gain some semblance of her old life. Having things in order around her seemed like a good start.

But there were much more important things to do, things like finding answers.

She'd have time to pick up these pieces later.

Trevor ushered her outside.

As soon as she stepped onto the porch, a car screech to a stop in front of them.

Then bullets fired.

———

"Get down!" Trevor shouted.

He started to reach for his gun.

Before he could grab it, he realized Sadie had reached for it.

She aimed it at the car and fired.

The back glass shattered.

A moment later, the car squealed away.

And Sadie stood there, an intense look on her face, almost as if she'd transformed into someone else.

As quickly as the expression had appeared, it vanished.

Her eyes and shoulders softened, and she lowered the gun.

Trembles overtook her.

Quickly, Trevor took the gun from her and shoved it into his holster. Then he placed his arm around Sadie.

"Are you okay?" he asked.

She nodded, still trembling. "Yes . . . I think so."

"Where did you learn to shoot like that?" It didn't make any sense . . . unless she was a trained assassin or something.

"I . . . I have no idea. It was all instinct."

"I'd say." He frowned as he replayed the incident.

That had been the last thing he'd expected.

Thankfully, no one had been hurt.

But that had been close.

His mind still reeled as he replayed what had happened.

Sadie definitely had some secrets.

For now, he called Detective Bennett. He needed to tell the man what had happened before the neighbors reported it.

But his heart was still racing as he tried to process Sadie's undeniable gun skills.

CHAPTER
SIXTEEN

DETECTIVE BENNETT CAME and took their statement.

He also collected evidence—the bullet casings. He took more photos. Talked to any neighbors who had security cameras.

Sadie had told him she was the one who'd fired. He would have seen that on the security footage anyway, so there was no need to cover it up.

He stayed a couple of hours before leaving.

Then she and Trevor climbed into his truck.

They hadn't really talked about what happened.

And she didn't want to.

How had she known to fire like that? What kind of instinct had kicked in?

She had no idea.

And that only confused her more.

Not only that but someone had shot at them in broad daylight!

What kind of person did that?

She knew. Someone who was desperate to silence her.

This was only the beginning.

"You want to talk?" Trevor asked.

She shook her head. "Not really. I don't know what to say."

"You still want to go to your office?"

"I do. We . . . I—I don't have any time to waste."

She found the company's website a few minutes later on her phone.

Then Trevor typed that address into his GPS, and they took off.

Maybe something there would trigger a memory . . . she could only hope.

Trevor had mixed feelings about going to Sadie's office building.

He wanted answers just as much as anyone.

But given everything that had happened, he didn't know who to trust.

He didn't know who *Sadie* could trust.

And he didn't know if he could trust Sadie.

What a mess.

Trevor didn't think she was faking her amnesia. If she was, then she should win some major acting awards. All her reactions seemed authentic and justified.

But then there were those gun moves . . . she'd been incredibly accurate and confident.

It didn't fit either Sadie he knew—the one before or after the accident. Not that she hadn't been confident. But she'd been an ordinary, everyday citizen.

Not a gun expert.

He only prayed this visit provided some answers.

He needed to know if she'd been lying to him.

If she had been lying, Trevor wanted to know why.

People who worked in his position and with his background had a lot at stake. There were many reasons why someone might want to use him—to get information, primarily.

Or, as Larchmont had suggested, one of his many enemies could be behind this. One of Trevor's colleagues was looking into that for him and seeing what kind of threats were out there.

Which was why Trevor had been so careful not to get too close to people. Danger always lurked nearby. It wasn't worth the risk.

But Sadie had seemed different.

He'd let himself start to hope that maybe a normal life was possible.

Now, it seemed as if his initial thoughts may have been wrong.

He felt Sadie's eyes on him and glanced from the small building to her. "Are you ready for this?"

"As ready as I'll ever be, I suppose. At least it's a small office, right? It's not like I'll have to sift through a hundred or so people."

"I looked it up earlier. There are only twenty-five employees who work here."

"Twenty-five employees? Seems manageable."

Trevor escorted her to the door and paused. "Ready?"

Sadie hesitated a moment before nodding to him. With her confirmation, he opened it, and they stepped inside.

CHAPTER
SEVENTEEN

A RECEPTIONIST SAT on the other side of the desk, a nameplate reading Stephanie Lansky in front of her.

The woman's eyes lit as soon as she saw them. "Sadie! I'm so glad you're okay. We've been so worried."

Stephanie quickly rounded the desk and pulled Sadie into a gentle hug.

Trevor watched as Sadie hugged the woman back, her motions marred with hesitancy.

Stephanie pulled away from Sadie but still held onto her arms. "I wasn't expecting to see you back so soon."

"I'm not here for work," Sadie said. "I was hoping to see my desk."

Realization flashed through Stephanie's gaze. "Of course. Let me just tell Frank you're here."

Trevor had done enough research to know that Frank Bolster was the owner of the business. The former pro golfer had started Sleeping Bear Elevator fifteen years ago and was now one of the leading elevator contractors in the area. The company did both commercial and residential sales and installation.

A moment later, a tall man with broad shoulders and an even broader belly stepped into the room.

"Sadie!" He grinned when he saw Sadie, but the smile quickly faded as he seemed to remember the circumstances. "I don't suppose you remember who I am."

"I only know Stephanie said your name was Frank and that you're my boss." Sadie's voice trembled, but just barely.

Trevor knew she was trying to hold it together.

"That's right. You're one of our valued employees here. I'm sure it will only be a matter of time before you regain your memory. In the meantime, I heard you want to see your office."

She nodded. "If you wouldn't mind."

"Of course not. Guy isn't here, by the way. He left about fifteen minutes ago to run an errand. I'm sure he would have stuck around if he knew you were coming."

Guy . . . the way Frank said the man's name made it sound like Guy and Sadie really did have a relationship.

An unsettled feeling jostled inside Trevor at the thought.

"Let me give everyone in the office a heads-up so they don't overwhelm you," Frank continued. "They're all going to be happy to see you after hearing what happened, but I'm sure you'll need some space. Let me talk to them, and I'll be right back to get you."

That seemed thoughtful, Trevor mused. Frank was worried about how Sadie might react to too much hoopla.

He had some questions for her coworkers. He either needed to find a way to talk to them on his own or to carefully word his inquiries around Sadie.

As he waited for Frank to return, he glanced at Sadie and saw the trepidation on her face. Anyone in her shoes would be nervous right now.

Though part of him was filled with compassion, his suspicions still remained.

She hadn't told him the truth. Why? What exactly had she lied about?

"Did you hear all the scuttlebutt in town?" Stephanie stared at them from behind her desk.

"Scuttlebutt?" Sadie asked.

Trevor braced himself. He'd known Sadie would eventually find out about what happened last night.

Was there ever a good time?

"A dead body was found in town yesterday." Stephanie's eyes sparkled as if she were proud of the juicy gossip she'd shared.

"A dead body?" Sadie repeated, blinking in confusion. "Whose? Not that I'll remember the name most likely."

"I haven't heard yet. Might be a tourist. Anyway, it's all people are talking about today. It's got everyone freaked out, especially after what happened to you."

Sadie looked up at Trevor. "Did you know about this?"

He nodded.

"You didn't tell me?" An edge of hurt quivered in her voice.

"I didn't think it was relevant."

Based on the stare she gave him, she didn't agree with him.

Before they could talk more, Frank reappeared, clearing it for them to come into the office.

Fear flashed on her face.

"You don't have to do this if you don't want to." Trevor kept his voice low as he said the words, not wanting Stephanie to overhear anything and spread information about Sadie.

Sadie shrugged then nodded. Then she shook her head as if she didn't know exactly how to respond. "I have to do this sometime. Why not now?"

Trevor had admired Sadie from the start. She'd had a fighting spirit when he'd first gotten to know her. It was part of what he liked about her.

He liked how she defended an elderly man in the hardware store when an employee had overcharged him. Liked how she had firm boundaries—like no man knowing where she lived until after the fourth date. Liked how she'd been sweet and playful.

All the most perfect combinations.

Sadie was still there. Only her memories had gone.

That thought brought Trevor a measure of comfort. He only hoped that Larchmont was wrong and that Sadie was exactly who she claimed to be.

The other part of him knew that his boss was rarely wrong.

Trevor hated that now more than ever.

———

Sadie ignored the tremble raking through her.

She shouldn't be so nervous. But she was.

What if Guy came back while she was here? What would she say to him?

Was he the man from her dream? The one that gave her warm, fuzzy feelings?

She didn't think so. Yet none of that reasoning was based on logic. It was all emotion.

She still had so much to sort through.

Trevor touched her elbow again, like he often did. She was grateful for his attention. Somehow it brought her back down to earth and made her feel like everything would be okay.

Again, something else that defied logic. But she needed that reassurance right now.

She paused once through the doorway leading into the office area and glanced around.

Six offices appeared to line the perimeter of the space, as well as a closet and bathroom. In the center of the building were eight small, partitioned cubicles. People sat at most of the desks, several of them glancing up at her with those looks in their eyes.

The looks of pity.

Sadie didn't have to remember these people to know the look.

In the back of the building was a small hallway with an Exit sign over it, probably a space set up for deliveries. Pictures of elevators and elevator shafts decorated the walls.

As Frank ushered her past the cubicles, people continued to give her looks and nods.

The responses probably came from a good place.

Who knew how to handle a situation like this? It wasn't addressed in some type of life manual or anything.

Sadie wouldn't hold it against anyone if they kept their distance, nor would she hold it against them that they had those looks of pity. She'd probably act the same in their shoes.

Frank opened a door for her and ushered her inside. "This is where you've worked for the past six months. You're a very dedicated employee. Always here on time. You often stay late, and you do good work."

"Six months?" Sadie assumed she'd been here longer.

"That's right," Frank said. "You were more than qualified for the job."

"Does my résumé say where I worked before this?"

"Somewhere in Ohio, I believe. I'll see if I can track down a copy of it." He nodded to another office. "In fact, I can go check now if you'd like."

"That would be great," she told him.

As he rushed away, a woman in her thirties with short blonde hair and a wide grin appeared in the doorway.

She stared at Sadie as if waiting for recognition. There was none.

"I'm April," the woman finally started. "Office

manager. I guess you don't remember me. I know Frank said not to bother you, but how could I not? We chatted all the time."

She realized April might be the perfect person to talk to. "No, it's okay. Could I ask you a few questions?"

"Of course."

"What can you tell me about myself? I know it sounds like a strange question, but anything could be helpful." Sadie noticed Trevor moved in closer as they talked. He wanted to hear this also.

"Oh, what's there to say? You're great to work with. You like salads from the deli down the street. You always talk about the beach. About how beautiful this area is." The animated woman's voice lilted as her hands flew through the air to emphasize every statement.

"Anything personal?"

April thought about it a moment before shrugging. "Not really. You've always been pretty private. You don't seem to like to talk about your past or anything."

Why was that? Sadie pondered. Because she was truly private? Or for other reasons?

"And Guy . . . ?" Sadie couldn't quite bring herself to finish the question.

April's eyes widened, and she nodded emphatically. "The two of you have definitely been hanging out."

"Hanging out or dating?" Sadie asked.

"I mean, everyone assumed you were dating. You never really clarified, I suppose."

Sadie hid a frown.

Why did the idea that she'd been dating Guy repulse her?

And what about the faint outline of blood she'd seen on her arm? And that man she'd seen walking into the hospital?

And the dead man discovered here in town?

Was everything connected?

Sometimes, Sadie felt certain she didn't want to know the answers.

CHAPTER
EIGHTEEN

TREVOR GLANCED AROUND THE OFFICE.

He knew his colleagues had been in here last night. They'd found that second phone under Sadie's desk.

Trevor also had two phones. Why? Because he was hiding something.

His jaw tightened. That was generally the reason why a person had two cells—to separate two parts of their lives.

So what was Sadie hiding? What other part of her life did she not want them to know about?

She looked spooked right now with her pale skin and shaky hands. Was that because of everything that had happened? Or were there other reasons? Did she remember a part of her life she didn't want to reveal?

Nothing seemed certain anymore, a fact that left him feeling unnerved.

As Sadie continued to chat with April, he scanned the people in the office. Two men popped their heads out of their offices—company executives if he had to guess. A delivery man walked through a back entrance, a dolly stacked with boxes in front of him.

Another man caught his eye, and Trevor sucked in a breath.

He'd seen that man last night. In the restaurant.

He had dark brown hair, a small build, and was probably in his sixties.

The name on his door read "Juan Blevins."

Was that a coincidence that another of Sadie's coworkers had been at that restaurant last night? Why hadn't he and Guy talked to each other?

Trevor supposed it was possible they hadn't seen each other.

But he stored that fact in the back of his mind.

Despite Frank's heads-up, everyone watched curiously.

Did any of these people have any answers?

There was only one way to find out.

By talking to them.

While Sadie and April continued to talk, he slipped away.

The woman sitting in the desk closest to Sadie's

office appeared to be an administrative assistant. She was in her fifties with salt-and-pepper hair to her chin and a quiet demeanor.

"Hi, there." Trevor plastered on his best smile. "I'm Trevor. I'm guessing you work with Sadie?"

The woman smiled back. "I'm Mary. And, yes, I do."

"We're trying to piece together parts of her life. As you probably know, she has amnesia."

The woman frowned. "I'm so sorry to hear that."

"When was the last time you saw her?"

"She stopped in yesterday morning but only for a second. She'd taken the rest of the day off, but she didn't say why. But I know she liked going to the beach, so I assumed that was it."

"She's only worked here for six months," Trevor continued. "Did she ever mention where she worked before that?"

"I think maybe she said she worked for some small company in Ohio."

"Ohio? Did she say if that's where she's from?" She was the second person to mention Ohio.

Mary shook her head. "That wasn't my impression, though she never really talked about her past much."

Another sign that Sadie could be hiding something. Trevor didn't want to believe it, but sooner or later he would have to face reality. All the facts were adding up.

"Any good friends here at the office?"

"Just Guy, I guess. But Sadie liked to keep to herself."

"I understand. Was she acting like herself yesterday morning when you saw her?"

Mary nodded. "I'd say so."

Trevor tried to put together a mental timeline.

If that man who'd been found dead in the woods —John Breckenridge—had been killed in the morning, would that have given Sadie enough time to come into work and then leave to meet Trevor at the beach?

He wasn't sure.

He remembered the blood he'd seen on her arm and hands. He'd already given Larchmont the towel so it could be tested.

It wouldn't tell them who had been hurt. Technology wasn't that advanced. But maybe they could match blood types. See if it belonged to the man who had died yesterday.

"There is one thing." Mary glanced around as if she didn't want anyone to hear.

"What's that?"

"As Sadie was walking past me yesterday, she dropped something." Her voice lowered to a whisper. "I picked it up and started to tell her, but she was already out the door. I figured I would give it to her when she came in yesterday, but then . . ."

"What was it?"

She opened her drawer and picked up something. Then she handed it to him. "It was a picture of this man. At first, I wondered if she was cheating on Guy."

As soon as Trevor saw the picture, he knew exactly who this man was.

It was John Breckenridge, the man who'd been murdered yesterday.

"Then I saw his picture on the news this morning," Mary whispered.

"Did you tell the police?"

Mary paused and then shook her head. "No. I thought about it. But Sadie helped me out when I didn't have money for my husband's heart surgery. She gave me some money. Told me I didn't have to repay her, even though I wanted to. I thought I at least owed it to her to keep this to myself . . . for now. You're her friend, right? You're looking into this?"

"I am."

"Then figure out why she had his picture. I don't want to get her in trouble. Can you do that for me?"

"I'd be happy to."

He slipped the photo into his pocket before anyone could see it.

What had Sadie been doing with a picture of the dead man?

Trevor didn't like any of the conclusions his mind wanted to draw.

As April scooted from the room, Sadie glanced at Trevor in the hallway.

Something had changed on his expression.

Had that woman he was talking to said something of interest?

She turned her gaze away before he saw her staring.

She'd been hoping for answers when she came here to the office. But now she felt as if she only had more questions.

She ran a hand along her desk, trying to picture herself sitting here crunching numbers. There were no personal items. No photos or inspirational quotes or awards she'd won.

The only thing that added any personality to the area were the colorful pens in a smiley face cup on her desk and a small, fake succulent beside it.

Why was it so hard for her to visualize herself working here?

She wasn't sure.

Realizing she had a moment to herself, she used her fingerprint to unlock her computer.

Her lungs felt frozen as she waited.

She wasn't sure what she expected to find, but her nerves felt tight enough to snap.

The screen lit, and she scanned the files on the desktop.

Nothing caught her eye. There were only invoices and other business-related things.

Nothing that sparked any type of memory.

She studied the file names.

Nothing looked suspicious or gave hints to anything.

Then again, what had she been expecting?

For fun, she clicked on the most innocuous files, one titled Invoices.

She began scrolling through the documents, but there was nothing of interest.

Until she spotted another folder in the Invoices folder.

One labeled: Invoices to be double-checked.

Sadie clicked on it.

Only invoices weren't inside.

It held photos.

Photos of . . . a tall man with white hair.

Her blood went cold.

Why in the world did she have pictures of this guy on her computer? Who was he?

Before she could ponder it longer, a shrill beeping sound filled the air.

Was that . . . an alarm?

Then she noticed the smoke lingering near the ceiling.

It was a smoke alarm, she realized.

The building was on fire.

CHAPTER
NINETEEN

TREVOR HEARD the alarm and stiffened.

"Is that what I think it is?" Sadie stood from her desk and rushed toward her office door.

"The fire alarm." Concern stretched across Frank's face as he hurried into the hallway. "We need to go. Everyone out!"

Employees stood from their cubicles, heads bobbing as they glanced around.

A thin layer of smoke already hovered near the ceiling.

"There!" Trevor pointed to a room at the back of the building. Smoke poured from it. "What's in there?"

"That's our supply closet," Frank said.

"You need to get everyone out of here!"

"Of course." Frank began ushering everyone toward an exit.

Trevor wanted to tell Sadie to go with them. But he didn't dare let her out of his sight. He didn't know who he could trust, and he wasn't taking any chances.

Instead, he rushed to the closet, her in tow.

He opened the door to make sure no one was inside.

It was clear.

But a small blaze crackled there.

He grabbed a fire extinguisher from the wall, pulled the pin, and sprayed the flames.

The fire shrank. Then, in the blink of an eye, it reignited—even stronger this time.

Someone had used an accelerant. He could smell gasoline.

He continued to spray the flames . . . until the extinguisher had nothing left inside.

He tossed it on the floor.

With a roar, the fire tripled in size.

Trevor rushed from the room, noting that everyone else had evacuated.

Good.

Then he glanced out a window toward the back of the property.

A lone figure ran toward the woods in the

distance. Based on the man's all-black attire, it wasn't an employee fleeing.

Most likely, it was the person who'd done this.

Had someone snuck inside through the back of the building and gone inside that closet to set a fire?

Was this related to what had happened to Sadie?

That was the only thing that made sense.

Someone had either wanted to distract them with that fire or they'd wanted to send another message.

Trevor wasn't sure which one.

But he didn't like either possibility.

"Trevor . . ."

He glanced back at Sadie and saw the fear in her gaze.

He grabbed her arm as the flames continued to spread. "We've got to get out of here!"

But Sadie froze. Didn't move at all.

Almost as if she'd gone into a trance.

Memories pummeled Sadie.

The scent of smoke. Of burning.

Of feeling helpless.

Her lungs tightened until she couldn't breathe.

She was trapped.

Couldn't get out.

She knew with certainty this place would be her grave.

"Sadie!" someone yelled.

Was that part of her memory? Or the present?

She had no idea.

But it didn't matter.

Either way, she could barely hear the voice over the flames.

She glanced around.

She stood in a room. A bedroom, she thought. Fire consumed all four walls and blocked the window.

"Help me!" she yelled.

But she knew no one could hear her.

The flames licked her skin, burning it. Smoke filled her lungs.

She was going to die!

Then, at once, someone lifted her.

Carried her.

The smell of smoke faded. The crackling softened.

Then she breathed fresh air.

Her feet touched the ground.

She heard her name again.

"Sadie?" a deep voice asked. "Can you hear me?"

Her eyes fluttered open.

She blinked.

Then she remembered where she was. What had happened.

Her office had been set on fire.

She and Trevor had raced out.

Then where was the room she'd been inside from her memories?

She blinked as Trevor's face came into view.

"Are you okay?" he rushed, concern etched around his eyes.

She blinked again, unsure. *Was* she okay?

"I . . . I don't know," she finally muttered.

"You're outside now. The fire isn't going to get you."

Her shoulders softened, and she tried to force her heart to slow.

"Did you have a memory?" Trevor still peered at her as sirens sounded in the background.

"I guess . . . may—maybe. I don't know." The throb in her head grew more intense.

"What happened?"

"I was a little girl, I think. Stuck in a house as it burned down. And . . ." She shrugged. "I felt helpless, like I knew I was going to die."

"You're not going to die." Trevor squeezed her arm. "You're okay."

If that was true, why did Sadie feel like nothing was okay? And like nothing would ever be okay again?

CHAPTER
TWENTY

SADIE SAT in Trevor's truck with the door open and a blanket around her shoulders.

Not that it was cold outside.

But she couldn't stop shivering.

Firefighters had arrived on the scene and put out the flames before they did too much damage.

But the fact remained that this fire had been set on purpose. She was unable to deny that.

Had someone wanted to distract her? To harm her?

She wasn't sure.

Detective Bennett had already arrived to question everyone. He started with her.

Trevor had helped to fill in some details Sadie was too shaken to remember.

When they finished, the detective moved on to

question other employees, and Trevor turned toward her, concern in his gaze. "I feel like you need to lie down and get some rest. You've been through a lot."

Something about the concern in his tone made her toes curl.

Her toes curl? She had to get a grip.

She shoved the thought aside and reminded him, "I don't have time. This isn't going to stop until we find answers."

"If you don't get some rest, your memories might not return." His voice sounded gentle and almost prodding instead of bossy. "You have to look at it that way as well."

Trevor's words made sense. But Sadie didn't want to slow down.

As they turned to climb into his truck, Sadie saw a man headed toward them. She'd seen him earlier.

The delivery driver, she realized.

He stopped in front of her before saying in a jovial voice, "Sadie, good to see you back."

She opened her mouth, unsure how to respond.

Trevor responded for her. "You may not have heard, but she was in an accident and lost her memory."

The man's eyes widened with surprise. "Oh, wow. I'm out for a couple of days, and I really did miss a lot. I'm sorry to hear that. I'm Bart."

Sadie offered a faint smile and nodded.

"You were making a delivery earlier, weren't you?" Trevor stepped closer.

"I was."

"Did you see anyone near the supply room?"

Bart pressed his lips together in hesitation. He paused another moment before glancing around. Then he stepped closer. "I wasn't going to say anything, but I did see Juan go inside as I was leaving."

"Who exactly is Juan?" Trevor asked. "What's his job here at the company?"

"He's the COO," Bart said. "He started here around the same time as Sadie."

Trevor's gaze darkened.

Did Juan have something to do with this?

Before she could say anything else, a car zoomed onto the scene. A black Mercedes that looked expensive—another weird fact she remembered. Why did she instinctively know which cars were pricey?

The door opened and . . . Guy stepped out.

Sadie's stomach sank.

His gaze went from the building to Sadie.

Then he rushed toward her, stopping entirely too close. At least he didn't touch her.

Bart scooted away, as if sensing an oncoming tense conversation.

"Are you okay?" Guy stared down at her.

Sadie nodded, wishing she could give him more. Especially if they truly had been dating.

But she couldn't right now. She didn't have it in her.

"Thankfully, no one was hurt," she told him.

"I can't believe this." He raked a hand through his hair and turned back toward the building. "What happened?"

Trevor filled him in. But Sadie noticed that as soon as Trevor spoke, some of Guy's friendliness disappeared.

Guy didn't like Trevor. Maybe he even felt intimidated by Trevor. Or jealous. She couldn't be sure.

Guy turned back to her, not hiding the fact he was shutting Trevor out. "Are you doing okay today? You look pale. Any progress?"

The barrage of questions made her chest tighten.

"Nothing really new," she finally said. "No new memories. I hoped going into the office might trigger something."

His shoulders seemed to slump. "That's too bad."

"Yes, it is disappointing."

Detective Bennett came to talk to Guy and led him away from Sadie.

She hated to admit it, but she was relieved to have space from him.

"How about this?" Trevor said. "I'll take you to the hotel. My colleague is already there with an adjoining room. You can take a nap. While you do that, I'll continue to research and see what I can find out. After you sleep for an hour or two, then we can continue trying to recover your memories."

A sense of relief swept through her, as it often did when she was with Trevor. His ideas always made sense, and he seemed to know what to suggest to keep her grounded. That confidence was exactly what Sadie needed right now.

"Okay," she finally said. "That sounds like a good plan."

———

Trevor took one last glance at Guy as he pulled away.

He couldn't help but notice that the man was wearing black and that the bottom of his dress shoes were muddy.

Could Guy have been the one Trevor saw running toward the woods after the fire started?

It seemed like a good possibility. But Trevor didn't want to bring it up. He didn't want to upset Sadie any more than she already was. She'd been through so much.

Instead, he kept the thought to himself—for now. He would share it soon enough. He would tell Kai and see what his colleague might be able to find out about the man. Trevor might even do some research of his own.

He even contemplated telling Detective Bennett. He just wanted to think everything through first.

The timing of Guy being out of the office was suspect. Maybe he'd left when he did on purpose. Had he somehow known Sadie was coming and planned this to either frighten or harm her?

That was the question Trevor had to ask himself.

What about that photo the administrative assistant had given him of the dead man? Why had Sadie been in possession of it?

He would eventually ask her—but not yet. Besides, it wasn't as if she would remember right now.

For now, Trevor needed to concentrate on getting Sadie away from here.

He didn't talk to her on the drive. He sensed she needed some time and space.

He sensed that because he knew her well enough to know that about her.

Another flash of guilt swept through him.

He wished he could tell her the truth. Could tell her that they did know each other.

But he remembered Larchmont's warning. Trevor would listen to his boss—at least until he had more information.

It didn't take long for them to reach the hotel Kai had booked for them.

It was a nice facility with interior hallways.

Trevor ushered Sadie upstairs, texting Kai on the way. His colleague met them in the hallway with the room keycard and let them inside.

Sadie wasted no time falling onto the bed.

"Can I get you anything before you rest?" Trevor asked.

Sadie shook her head, her eyelids starting to sag with exhaustion. "No, I just need to sleep."

Trevor would let her do that. When she awoke, he'd get her something to eat. He wanted to look out for her. She needed someone right now, and he wanted to be that person.

"I'll just be in the next room." He turned the lights off and walked into the adjoining room.

He and Kai needed to talk. Kai had been looking into some things, and now Trevor wanted to know what his colleague had found out. But they'd need to keep their voices down. For more than one reason.

Trevor sat at the corner table and glanced at Kai. "Anything?"

"I put together a list of about eight people you might have made mad enough to do this for revenge," Kai started. "I looked into each of them. Checked for alibis. Of course, most of these people have a small army at their disposal, any of which they could have hired to do their dirty work."

"Anyone stand out or raise any red flags?"

He reached into his pocket and handed Trevor a paper. "Just one. Frederick Moreau. I wrote up everything I could find about him here."

"Frederick Moreau?" Frederick was the last person Trevor had expected Kai to mention.

The man had been running an intricate human-trafficking organization.

He was deplorable.

But Trevor had managed to collect a thick file of evidence on the man and what he was doing. He'd turned it into the authorities, Frederick had been arrested, and his operation shut down last year.

But that didn't mean he didn't have minions willing to get revenge for him.

"There's been some chatter in the prison that he'd been plotting something," Kai continued. "And everyone knows he hates you."

"That he does." Frederick had made that abundantly clear as he'd been arrested. He'd been on the verge of getting away—and slipping off somewhere he'd probably never be found.

Frederick would have probably had his men start up little "enterprises" whenever he saw fit. His crime reign would have continued.

Trevor had pretended to be one of his guys, and Frederick had let him into his circle.

When Trevor betrayed him, Frederick vowed revenge.

"You think he may have sent someone to the beach to go after me, but this person hit Sadie instead?"

Kai eyed him a moment before shrugging. "I suppose that's one theory."

Kai knew there was more going on. That was evident.

But Trevor couldn't explain everything. Instead, he asked, "Anything else?"

Kai sighed. "Sadie Carrington appears to be a carefully made-up persona. Whoever put together her background is good. I almost didn't catch several things."

"Bennett said her fingerprints checked out."

"Like I said, whoever put this together is good. I'm still trying to find out who she really is."

Normally, if Trevor was going to break the rules and date someone, he would have looked into her background.

Instead, this time he'd thrown caution to the wind.

Had that been a deadly mistake?

CHAPTER
TWENTY-ONE

TREVOR FELT Kai's eyes on him and quickly tried to clear his expression.

"Why do you look so upset?" his colleague asked.

Trevor forced his shoulders to appear casual as he shrugged. "Sadie just doesn't seem like the type to live a lie."

Kai continued to eye him. "But remember . . . you don't know her very well."

"No, I don't," Trevor conceded.

"For all we know, she could be in witness protection. The government could have easily fabricated fingerprints for her in the system and created a new background."

"Maybe." Trevor hadn't really thought about that possibility.

Kai tilted his head. "Are you going to ask her?"

Trevor gave his colleague a sharp glance. "You think she's faking her amnesia?"

He shrugged. "It's a possibility. We should consider everything. It's only wise."

Trevor couldn't argue with Kai's statement, even if he didn't want to believe it. Instead, he let out a sigh. "I think asking her would be premature. But I'll keep the possibility in the back of my mind. In the meantime, I want to look into Guy more. Something about him bothers me."

Kai opened his computer and typed in a few things. "I did a preliminary check, but nothing came up. He's thirty-five. Been married once. Worked in various sales jobs throughout the area."

"I'm going to dig deeper. There's got to be more to Guy."

"I also looked into some other people at the office. The one person who sparked the most suspicion was April."

"I met her today. What about her?"

"She's had a couple of arrests—one for drunk driving. Another for shoplifting. Those were quite a few years ago. What concerns me the most is her relationship with a man named Joseph Hayden. He's a known drug dealer."

"Interesting . . . see what else you can find out on him. And while you're at it, dig a little deeper in Juan Blevins also."

"Will do."

"If we don't find some answers, these people will just keep coming after Sadie."

Kai nodded before rubbing his neck. "The whole situation is strange. If it turns out not to be Guy, maybe Sadie has an ex-boyfriend. You know what they say? The root of most crimes is love or money."

Trevor let that settle for a minute. Kai was right. Most crimes *were* motivated by those things.

Sadie had never mentioned a crazy ex-boyfriend.

Then again, she hadn't mentioned Guy either.

Nothing was as it seemed.

Had Trevor been a fool to believe her innocence? Or should he continue to give her the benefit of the doubt?

Sadie sat up in bed with a start.

Her heart stampeded in her chest. Sweat covered her brow.

She glanced around, panic filling her.

Where was she?

She soaked in the white walls. The long dresser. The TV hanging over it.

A hotel room, she realized. But how had she gotten here?

Then she remembered.

Trevor had brought her here to rest while they figured things out.

She let out a breath and slumped back down in bed.

Then she tried to search back farther in her thoughts and hit a figurative wall.

That was right. She'd lost her memory.

Had her nap stirred any thoughts?

Sadie kept trying to conjure information about her past. But there was nothing. Empty pages. A screen with only static. A canvas painted white.

How was this even possible? She could understand her brain blocking out the event where she was almost killed. But why was her brain blocking out the rest of her memories? It didn't make sense.

She supposed that was how the brain worked sometimes. She *had* hit her head hard.

In fact, according to the doctor, she was lucky to be alive.

Movement across the room caught her eye, and she saw Trevor step into the doorway.

Just the sight of him loosened her lungs.

Even though he was hired help, Sadie felt as if she could depend on him. Maybe because he had been the one person who'd been there for her since this ordeal started.

She prayed her trust wasn't misplaced.

"How was your nap?" He leaned in the doorway,

his hands casually tucked into the pockets of his jeans.

She averted her gaze as her cheeks heated.

Those thoughts . . . they weren't appropriate. The two of them only had a professional relationship—there was no room for attraction.

"I guess it was pretty good. I don't remember much." She let out a dry laugh. "Usually, that's a good thing, but I suppose in my case . . ."

He offered a compassionate smile. "Your case is a tough one."

She let out another breath. No one knew that better than her.

"What now?" She ran a hand through her hair, hoping it didn't look too crazy.

"Are you hungry? I thought we could get a late lunch/early dinner."

"Now that you mention it, I *am* hungry."

"Anything sound good?"

"A burger and fries." Then she paused. "Isn't that strange? How do I know that sounds good? That a burger and fries are something I like?"

He shrugged. "I certainly can't explain it."

"That makes both of us. Just let me get freshened up."

CHAPTER
TWENTY-TWO

A FEW MINUTES LATER, Sadie had touched up her makeup and hair, and she was ready to go.

They stepped outside, and Sadie saw Trevor glancing around again. Always on guard. She was thankful to know he took this seriously.

"I looked up some restaurants while you were in the bathroom, and I think I found one that will work," Trevor told her as they walked across the parking lot. "It's a local establishment."

"Those are always the best."

"Then let's head to Burger Haven."

Trevor helped her into his truck before climbing in himself. The restaurant was only five minutes away, not far enough to establish any type of real conversation.

Thankfully, they were between the lunch and

dinner rushes and were seated right away. Without looking at the menu, Sadie knew she wanted a bacon cheeseburger, fries, and a Cherry Coke.

Again, so strange. But she wasn't arguing. At least it was *something*.

The waitress appeared to take their order and paused. She glanced back and forth between the two of them, an unreadable look in her eyes.

"Is everything okay?" Trevor narrowed his gaze as he observed the woman.

She popped out a hip and tilted her head. "Oh, it's fine. Good to see you both again."

Sadie squinted. "You must have us mistaken for someone else."

Confusion flashed in her gaze. "Didn't the two of you come in here last week?"

"No," Sadie said. "Why would you ask?"

The waitress twisted her lips. "I thought I remembered seeing the two of you. You guys looked so happy that it was memorable. I was a little jelly."

"We weren't in here last week," Trevor told her.

The waitress still looked unconvinced, but she shrugged. "Weird. Anyway, can I take your order?"

As Sadie and Trevor placed their order, Sadie's phone dinged.

It was Frank. He'd emailed her a copy of her résumé.

That would be a nice distraction from the strange conversation with the waitress.

She tried to imagine being here with Trevor last week. The thought was laughable—yet intriguing.

If only it were true.

Trevor's thoughts raced.

Coming here had been a mistake.

The truth was, he and Sadie *had* been here last week.

He didn't think anyone would recognize them. But he'd hoped being here would trigger something for Sadie.

Thankfully, Sadie didn't seem to think much about what the waitress had said—and now they had the résumé to distract them.

Sadie showed it to Trevor, and they both read through it together.

She'd attended Purdue. Graduated Magna Cum Laude. Worked for a large accounting firm in Cleveland. Then she'd taken this job in Michigan.

"Anything stick out to you?" Trevor asked. "Trigger any memories?"

She frowned and shook her head. "I can't say it has."

"That's too bad."

She sat up straighter. "Oh, by the way, there *was* one thing in the office I was going to tell you about, but the fire alarm interrupted us."

He perked. "What's that?"

"I found this semi-hidden folder on my computer. There wasn't much inside, except pictures of a man with thick, white hair."

Trevor kept his expression even. "Anything else distinguished about him?"

"The photos appeared to be taken when the man was unaware. I have no idea who he is."

"Maybe we can get a copy and run it through the system."

She nodded. "Good idea."

Trevor shifted, trying to figure out how to approach the next subject. Finally, he asked, "Mary, your administrative assistant, said you dropped this photo yesterday morning."

He pulled the picture from his pocket and slid it across the booth to her.

"Do you recognize this man?" he asked.

She stared at the face there before shaking her head. "I can't say that I do. Who is he?"

"He's the man who was killed yesterday."

Her eyes widened, and her words came out just above a screech. "What? Why would I have his photo?"

"I have no idea."

She rubbed her throat as if fighting panic. "What if I *did* have something to do with that man's death? I couldn't live with myself if that turned out to be true."

"We'll get to the bottom of this," Trevor reassured her.

Silence fell between them a moment, and Trevor let her have some time.

Finally, he said, "This is the part where I would usually ask you questions about yourself."

The corner of his lips curled in an apologetic grin.

Sadie let out a clipped laugh. "I know. It's a little hard to get to know me if I don't even know myself."

Her words sounded strained.

Then her gaze flitted up to his. "I guess we could talk about you."

He shrugged. "Not much to say really. I'm pretty boring. I mostly work. Actually, I work entirely too much. I'm trying to change that, but it's not easy."

"I can imagine."

Trevor's gaze stopped on something outside, and his lungs tightened. A man lingered behind a truck.

Staring at the restaurant.

No, staring at them.

Trevor rose. "Stay here."

Then Trevor took off running, determined to catch the man and learn what he was up to.

CHAPTER
TWENTY-THREE

TREVOR RUSHED THROUGH THE RESTAURANT, paused on the sidewalk, and glanced around.

Where had the man gone?

Movement across the parking lot caught his eye.

It was him! The man who'd been watching him at the restaurant last night. The one who'd shot at him.

Trevor took off after him. But the man had too much of a head start.

Earlier today, he'd wondered if Guy had been the man running away from the fire at the office. But this man didn't have Guy's build.

Was there more than one person involved in this ordeal?

That was Trevor's best guess.

But that only made this whole situation even more complicated.

The man continued to dodge parked cars. Trevor stayed behind him, quickly closing in.

The next instant, a blue sedan with dark windows pulled to a screeching halt in front of the man.

The guy jumped into the back.

Then the car squealed away, blowing through a red light, causing several drivers to lay on their horns and throw on their brakes.

Trevor committed the license plate to memory, though he knew it probably wouldn't do much good. If this was the same person who'd hit Sadie, he'd known to steal a vehicle and then ditch it. It would probably be the same case this time.

Just like the person who'd called Sadie yesterday but said nothing. It had been an untraceable burner.

Trevor watched as the vehicle disappeared, his muscles hard.

He shouldn't have let the man get away. If that car hadn't pulled up to help the man escape, he wouldn't have. Trevor would have chased this man until he caught him.

For now, he stalked back to the restaurant.

He committed what the man looked like to memory. The guy had worn all black, including his hat. His clothing made it nearly impossible to distinguish any of his features. But Trevor saw some light-brown hair peeking out from beneath his baseball cap.

A touch of relief filled him when he saw that Sadie was okay—although she looked terrified as she sat wide-eyed at the table.

Their food had been delivered, but she hadn't touched hers.

He slid into the booth across from her. "He got away."

"I know. I saw everything." She frowned. "Anything about him catch your eye?"

Trevor shook his head. "I got a few more details but not much. At least two people are working together because someone picked this guy up."

"I don't like the sound of that." Sadie rubbed her arms as if chilled.

"Me neither. Don't worry, we're going to keep looking into this."

"Thank you. I appreciate all you're doing for me."

"It's my job. It's what I'm paid to do." Trevor immediately regretted the words, especially when he saw the red flash across her cheeks.

For some reason, it felt necessary to say those words to create distance.

But he didn't mean what he said. He would have stayed here to help her, even if she hadn't hired him. In fact, no one would be able to keep him away.

He cared about her. That much was obvious.

Except now he really had no idea who this woman was.

Strange how twenty-four hours could turn everything upside down.

Sadie picked at her burger and fries, trying to force herself to eat. The food was tasty, but her appetite had disappeared.

Trevor, on the other hand, ate everything in front of him before pushing his plate away. That was a good thing. He needed the nourishment if he wanted to keep up his energy.

He took the check and pulled some cash from his wallet.

She didn't bother to argue this time.

However, unless she regained some memories, she wouldn't have a job. She would need a way to earn a living.

The unknowns battered her a moment until she pushed them away.

She'd figure that out later.

It's my job. It's what I'm paid to do.

His words slammed back into her mind, and she cleared her throat.

She was so thankful he'd been the one to save her.

That he'd stuck around to check on her. That he happened to work for a security group.

If she believed in coincidences, then she might think that was what had occurred. But she believed things happened for a purpose. She believed her path had crossed with Trevor's for a reason.

We know that all things work together for the good of those who love God: those who are called according to His purpose.

More Scripture popped into her mind, seeming to confirm to Sadie that she was a believer.

Did she go to church around here? Would that be a way to find answers?

It was something to think about.

"What now?" Sadie asked after the waitress returned with his change.

Trevor let out a long breath. His muscles were taut—and nicely bulky as his arms rested on the table. His gaze was intense and intelligent. His cheek twitched with thought.

The man really was handsome.

She wanted to know more about him, about how he'd gotten to this place in his life.

But this didn't seem like the right time to ask.

"I'm trying to think of other places I could take you to regain some of your memories," Trevor finally said. "We've been to your house and to your workplace."

"April at the office mentioned that I liked to go to the beach. Maybe if we went back to the scene where this all happened, I could remember something." Sadie knew she was probably getting desperate. But she was willing to throw whatever necessary at the wall to see what stuck.

Trevor studied her with concern in his gaze. "Do you think that's a good idea?"

Sadie shrugged. "I don't see where it could hurt. There's a good chance I'm not going to remember anything anyway."

"But if you do, it could be . . . traumatic."

"If it traumatizes me, then I know you'll handle it. You'll take me to the hospital if that's what needs to happen. I don't want to relive the horror of being hit by that car, but I need to remember my past."

Trevor stared at her another moment as if contemplating her words. Finally, he nodded. "Then let's do it."

Several seconds later, they took off in his truck again.

Sadie studied the landscape around her as they drove. The trees. The sandy earth. But just as expected, nothing looked familiar or triggered any memories.

Finally, twenty minutes later, they pulled into the parking lot. A sick feeling swirled inside her.

This was where it happened. Where her whole life had changed.

When she saw the lot, however, nothing triggered her.

She felt nothing. Nothing at all.

Trevor parked in a space one row back and pointed to an area near a walkover. "That's where the car hit you."

Sadie stared at it, still feeling nothing except anxiety. "It's all blank."

He nodded grimly. "I'm sorry."

Disappointment bit deep. She'd thought if anything could trigger a memory, it would be coming here.

But her memories were all still a sea of emptiness, vast and deeper than the massive, ocean-like lake in front of her.

"I want to look around," she murmured.

"Of course."

They climbed out and walked toward the dunes. Near a walkover, she paused and imagined everything playing out.

Imagined herself standing there with a beach bag. Imagined herself seeing a car hurtling toward her. Imagined the fear she must have felt.

Imagined herself lying on the ground and then waking up, having no recollection of what had happened.

She sucked in a shaky breath before studying the ground around her, looking for anything the police may have missed. She wasn't sure what she expected to find. Still, it seemed worthwhile to look around, just in case.

At that thought, something nestled in a crevice in the pavement caught her eye. She gingerly picked it up.

"What's that?" Trevor stepped closer.

She squinted. "I'm not sure how I know this, but it almost looks like . . . one of those earpiece things. You know, like one of those things that could be used by cops during a sting operation or something."

He leaned closer for a better look. "I think you're right. Or someone jogging could have dropped it while listening to some music."

"You're right." She laughed at herself. "Of course. That's probably what it is. It's probably not even mine."

But, even as she said the words, she didn't believe them.

Something about the small electronic device in her hands felt familiar, though she wasn't sure why.

Just in case, she slipped it into her pocket.

CHAPTER
TWENTY-FOUR

TREVOR AND SADIE walked to the shore to stare out at the water.

That earpiece she'd found?

It was totally something an operative would use and definitely not something for recreational use.

Trevor didn't want to tell her that, however.

Had it been Sadie's? Or had someone else been lingering close during the accident and dropped it?

Trevor didn't know, but he didn't like the possibilities floating in his mind.

He wanted desperately for Sadie to remember.

Except he didn't.

Because he still had no idea how he would explain why he wasn't telling her about their relationship.

It bugged him, which didn't make sense. He lived

a life of subterfuge. He'd taken on the roles of many different people. He'd pretended to be a politician once. A scientist another time. Once he'd even posed as a lion tamer.

Usually when he took on those roles, it wasn't at the expense of anyone he cared about. In fact, he'd been carefully trained not to care about anyone and to focus only on the mission.

It was what made operatives good at their jobs. That was what Larchmont always said.

For so long, Trevor had believed him. His whole life had revolved around his work.

But lately, he'd been questioning things. Wanting more. Feeling as if his thoughts and actions had been programmed.

Then there were the tremors he'd been experiencing lately. They came and went at random times.

Larchmont claimed it was a result of some of the battles he'd fought and how hard they'd been on the body.

Trevor wasn't sure he agreed.

He and his colleagues had practically been lab rats as they were made into super soldiers for the government. He was nearly certain that he wasn't aware of most of the experiments he'd been put through.

One day, he would get to the bottom of it.

He and Sadie stayed on the shore, the breeze

blowing on their faces. She stared out at the lake as if it might have the answers she needed.

The best thing Trevor could give her was silence. Filling up quiet with meaningless conversation would only delay her healing process. He knew that firsthand.

He'd suffered some significant injuries on two of his jobs. He'd thought he might even lose a leg once. Thankfully, everything had healed. But those days had been rough.

He scanned the area again.

Whoever had done this was most likely still trailing them. But Trevor had been careful on the way here. He hadn't seen anyone following his truck. He'd even looked for trackers and hadn't found any.

How had that guy found them at the restaurant?

He was missing something.

He needed to investigate this situation further. Until then, he would remain on guard.

Sadie's life depended on it.

―――

Sadie was thankful for the quiet. Thankful Trevor seemed to know what she needed right now.

She settled on the empty beach and pulled her knees to her chest as she stared at the water. The day was warm—probably in the low eighties—and the sun covered her shoulders and face. Being here felt therapeutic.

She tried to imagine herself in this very spot earlier. Tried to imagine herself enjoying being on the shore.

Did she usually go in the water? Sunbathe? Have picnics? Bonfires?

She had no idea, nor was she sure how much longer she could live like this. What if she never regained her memories?

The thought caused a cry to rise up in her.

She quickly cleared her throat before Trevor sensed her despair. He tended to be able to do that. Sometimes it seemed as if he could even predict what she would say or do next.

Why was that? Was he this intuitive with everyone?

She found it both comforting and unnerving.

She needed to be strong. Not because Trevor had told her that. But because there would be time to fall apart later—after she had answers.

She stole a glance at him. Saw the sunlight glinting on his hair. Saw the intense look in his eyes as he stared at the water.

At once, an image hit her. A memory?

She didn't know.

Her mind jerked back in time at a dizzying speed.

Felt as if she'd had this moment before.

Like she and Trevor had sat on this shore and shared this exact instant.

Then she blinked, and whatever it was—a memory or her imagination—disappeared.

Was it déjà vu?

"Sadie?" Trevor stared at her.

She ran a hand over her eyes, her head suddenly beginning to pound.

That moment couldn't have been right. She'd just been imagining things. Having a daydream.

She and Trevor had never been here together before . . . right?

"Sadie? Are you okay?" Trevor scrutinized her even more deeply.

What should she say? Did she pretend like she hadn't had that memory? That blip in her thoughts?

Or should she be forthcoming?

She licked her lips, unsure what was the best play to make.

Finally, she asked, "Are you sure you and I have never met before this incident? Even briefly, maybe?"

He stared at her, and for just a split second a shadow filled his gaze. As quickly as the emotion appeared, it was gone, leaving her to wonder if she'd imagined it.

"No, ma'am," he finally said. "Like I said, I'm only here for a few days on vacation."

She let out a feeble, self-deprecating laugh and nodded. "Right."

"Why do you ask?" His voice sounded even—unoffended and absent of curiosity. All logic and reasoning.

Sadie shrugged. "It's . . . nothing. It was just this feeling I got."

The shadow crossed his gaze again.

Was he lying? Hiding something? Could Sadie even trust this man?

What if his presence in her life wasn't something that was ordained at all?

What if they'd been thrown together because he had something to do with what was going on?

Sadie's gut twisted at the thought. She didn't want the idea to be true.

But she also couldn't rule out any possibility, not when her life was on the line.

So exactly who could she trust?

She knew the answer: no one.

CHAPTER
TWENTY-FIVE

TREVOR TRIED NOT to stare at Sadie.

But she'd had a memory of some sort, hadn't she?

Had she remembered him?

A lump formed in his throat.

At once, he wanted to explain. To tell her everything. To reassure her that she wasn't losing her mind.

But he couldn't do any of those things. He'd promised Larchmont he'd find out information on Sadie and keep his real identity—as well as their previous relationship—quiet. At what point should his loyalty switch from Larchmont to himself?

He'd vowed to be his own person, yet he felt a sense of duty to the Shadow Agency. It was all he'd known for so long—first loyalty to the military and then to Larchmont.

But there was more to life than his job. What would it take for him to make the change? He wasn't sure, but he was tempted to give it a try.

He averted his gaze and clamped his mouth shut before he told Sadie something he shouldn't.

Abruptly, Sadie stood and wiped the sand from her jeans. "I think we should go."

Concern filled him as he jumped to his feet. "Is everything okay?"

"I'm suddenly not feeling well." Her voice sounded pinched with tension.

"Do I need to take you back to the doctor?" He'd been afraid she might have a trauma response to being here.

Sadie shook her head. "It's not like that. It's just . . . I just need to be away from here."

Or did she mean she needed to be away from *him*?

Before they could talk more, she hurried toward the truck.

Trevor lunged forward and grabbed her arm. As soon as he touched her, she swirled around, something flashing in her gaze.

Was that fear?

His chest tightened. The last thing he wanted was to frighten Sadie more.

He released her arm and raised his hands. "I need to go ahead of you in case trouble is waiting for us."

Sadie's shoulders seemed to relax with understanding. Trevor moved in front of her, surveying the parking lot for any signs of danger.

He wouldn't let these guys get to her again. He would do everything in his power to protect her—like he should have protected her the first time.

When he saw nothing suspicious nearby, he released a long breath.

"Let's go." He led Sadie to his truck, and they climbed inside.

She still looked on edge, and he wished there was a way to reassure her.

As he snapped his seatbelt in place, he wondered what he could say. But without knowing what had rattled her, nothing came to mind.

Before he could force any awkward conversation, Sadie's phone rang.

"It's Detective Bennett," she murmured.

Sadie answered and put the phone on speaker.

"I need you to come down to the office," Detective Bennett said. "I have an update I'd rather not share on the phone."

Sadie's eyes widened. "O . . . okay. We'll be right there."

Based on the tone of the detective's voice, he had bad news.

Trevor could only imagine what that might be.

Sadie was nearly certain she'd vomit as she stepped into the police station.

What if Bennett shared something she didn't want to hear?

Why would she even think that? The detective might have good news.

Maybe she should be happy.

But instead, her nerves zinged around inside her like an electrical wire that had been cut and now zapped everything it touched.

Why did she have this sense of foreboding? Maybe it was her subconscious's way of telling her she'd been doing something illegal before all this happened.

Was she a criminal? Sure, she hadn't been arrested before, but that didn't mean she hadn't committed a crime. It might just mean she hadn't been caught.

She had no idea what she'd done in the past. She could only guess.

The faint streaks of blood she'd found on her arm in the hospital flashed back in her mind. If it wasn't her blood, whose was it?

Had the detective connected her to a violent crime?

Her thoughts continued to tumble around, making her feel sicker and sicker.

Detective Bennett met them at the front desk and motioned for them to follow him down a short hallway and into a small room.

An interrogation room.

Her throat went dry.

Trevor paused by the door. "Would you like for me to wait out here?"

That was a good question. If only Sadie knew she could trust him. If only anything made sense to her.

She should say no. That was the safest choice.

But the truth was, she *did* want Trevor here to help her sort out anything the detective might share. To be a listening ear. An objective companion.

After a moment of contemplation, she finally nodded toward the room. "If you wouldn't mind joining me, that would be great."

She knew one thing for certain. If she and Guy truly were dating, by the end of this, they most likely wouldn't be. She'd basically shut the man out. Even though she thought she should feel bad about it, she didn't.

She didn't want Guy with her right now.

She wanted Trevor—a fact that left her feeling unbalanced.

Trevor stepped inside the interrogation room and sat next to her in a metal chair in front of a grungy wooden table.

"Thanks again for coming." Detective Bennett

propped his arms on the table and leaned toward her.

"Is this interrogation room really necessary?" Trevor asked.

"It's just the easiest place to meet," Bennett explained, his voice casual.

But was it? Sadie had a hard time believing that.

"We talked to some of your neighbors to see if they might know something," Bennett continued. "The consensus was that you're friendly but keep to yourself a lot of the time."

"Okay . . ." She rubbed her palms against her jeans, wondering where he was going with this.

"There was one neighbor that said she saw you arguing with someone about a week ago."

Surprise—and hope—rushed through her. Maybe this was something that could give her a clue about who had run her down.

"What else did she say?" Sadie rushed. "Could she hear what the argument was about?"

The corners of Bennett's lips flickered down in a frown. "Unfortunately, no. But she said it was heated."

"Who was I arguing with?"

"A man she'd never seen before."

"Could it have been Guy?" Trevor suggested.

Bennett shrugged as if dismissing the idea. "Your neighbor said he was a short man with darker skin. He doesn't fit Guy's description, nor does he fit the description of anyone you work with."

Disappointment bit at her. "Then who could it have been?"

"The man *does* fit one description," Bennett announced.

"Who's that?"

Bennett slid a picture across the table toward her. "Him."

She glanced at the photo, flinching at the image there.

It was the same man Trevor had shown her. Only he'd been alive in the other picture.

In this photo he was . . . dead. Eyes closed. Skin pale. Body lifeless. Metal morgue slab behind him.

She pressed her eyes closed, nausea churning inside her.

"I know that's hard to see, but it's all we've got," Bennett said. "Anything trigger a memory?"

She pulled her eyes open and glanced at the photo one more time before looking away and shaking her head.

No flashes of recognition had hit her.

Should she tell him about that other photo?

She didn't know.

But her gut told her not to. She didn't want to keep information from the police. But she needed more answers first. Otherwise, she could be sealing her own prison sentence.

"I'm sorry, but he's not familiar to me." The words were true.

Bennett nodded stoically but said nothing else. He simply put the photo back into a folder he had with him.

"Who is he?" Trevor asked.

"He's the man who turned up dead around the same time as your accident."

Sadie pressed her eyes shut. She'd known that was the truth. But hearing the detective say the words aloud drove home the reality of the situation.

And it was dire.

CHAPTER
TWENTY-SIX

TREVOR REFLECTED on what he knew.

Sadie had been seen arguing with a man who, according to Larchmont, had said he'd come to town to kayak. That man had later turned up dead.

When Trevor had found Sadie, she'd had blood on her hands.

The dead man had been stabbed.

There had to be more to this story—but they may not ever know the rest until Sadie's memory returned.

Trevor turned his attention back to Bennett, curious as to what the man knew. From the sounds of it, Larchmont was several steps ahead of the detective in this investigation.

"Has the murder weapon been found?" Trevor asked.

"Not yet," Bennett said. "We're still looking."

"Do you know this man's identity?" Trevor continued.

"No, unfortunately he's another mystery. His fingerprints haven't turned up anything. We just released his image to the press earlier. Then when we realized his image matched that of a man seen arguing with Ms. Carrington . . ."

A twinge of guilt filled Trevor when he realized he already knew the man's name. Larchmont had been able to find out.

But Trevor kept that information to himself for now. If Trevor admitted how much he knew, it could raise suspicions.

"Are you arresting me?" Sadie asked.

"Because you were seen arguing with our dead man?" Bennett raised his brow again. "Unfortunately, there's not enough evidence to hold you."

"Unfortunately?" Trevor's gaze narrowed.

What an odd word choice. It was almost as if the detective *wanted* to arrest Sadie. Otherwise, why would he say that?

Bennett rubbed the back of his neck, appearing exhausted. "We're examining every possibility as we try to figure out what's going on."

"You think I killed that man?" Sadie's voice sounded raspy with fear.

Bennett dropped his hand from the back of his neck and locked gazes with her. "It is strange that the same day you were hit and lost your memory, this man turned up dead approximately two miles away."

"That doesn't mean she had anything to do with it." Protectiveness rose in Trevor's voice.

"No, it doesn't." But the detective didn't sound convinced.

He was looking for answers. No doubt the people above him were pressing the man for answers. Citizens were probably scared.

"Is that all you need?" As far as Trevor was concerned, this conversation was over.

"For now." But Bennett's brow rippled, promising he would have more questions as he continued to dig deeper.

Trevor stood and motioned for Sadie to follow. If she talked any more, she'd need a lawyer present.

There were clearly parts of Sadie's life he wasn't aware of.

It made sense. He and Sadie hadn't known each other that long.

He had secrets due to his line of work.

But she also had secrets of her own. Big secrets. Dangerous secrets.

What was she hiding? Whatever it was, she'd had parts of her life she'd kept from him. Parts of her life that maybe she didn't want him to know, possibly for less-than-honorable reasons.

He crossed his arms as they left the office. He didn't like the thought of that.

Who was Sadie Carrington? Who was she *really*?

Certainly, the police had run all the background checks on her.

Had they figured out she was living under a false identity? Trevor didn't think so. If they knew that, Bennett showed no signs of it.

Things just didn't add up in his mind, and Trevor needed to figure out what to do about it.

He and Sadie climbed back into his truck and sat there a moment. Trevor gave her the chance to speak without worrying about whether the detective or another officer might overhear.

"I'm ready to go back to the hotel." Her voice sounded soft—almost strained—as she said the words.

He understood. It had been a long day, and that meeting with Bennett had been a doozy.

"Just because you may have been seen arguing with that man who died doesn't mean you had anything to do with his death."

"Doesn't mean I didn't either," she muttered.

"We'll figure this out."

A smile fluttered across her lips. "Thanks. I appreciate that."

Before he could put his truck into Reverse, her phone rang again. She glanced at the screen and frowned.

"Everything okay?" Trevor asked.

"It's Guy. He's called a couple of times, but I haven't answered. Is that terrible?"

"No, it's your choice. Do you want to talk to him now?"

"I don't know." She shrugged, but her voice sounded listless.

"You don't have to do anything you're not comfortable with. You have a lot of healing to do, and you need to do things on your terms. Don't let other people dictate how you handle this."

She glanced over and offered a tight smile as if his words had brought a small measure of relief. "Thanks. You always seem to know what to say."

"Not always. But I try. I really can't imagine what I'd do in your shoes. How are you holding up? Really?"

"My thoughts are like a jumbled ball of yarn. Every once in a while I feel like I get one knot out, but there are still hundreds waiting for me. Then while I'm trying to get another knot worked out, the first knot somehow materializes again."

What did that mean? Had she had a memory she hadn't shared with him?

Trevor knew he couldn't press her. Sadie would share any realizations with him on her terms.

Plus, he needed to figure out what he would tell her if she did regain her memories. How would he explain his deceit?

The truth was, there was nothing he could say to make the situation right. There was no good excuse for his deception, none that Sadie would accept—or even that she *should* accept.

Following Larchmont's orders had sealed the fate of their relationship. No solid foundation could be built upon secrets and lies.

Even if she understood why he'd done what he had, Trevor wondered if he'd even want a relationship with Sadie. She'd also been deceiving him, and he had no idea why.

But he was determined to find out, and that meant staying close.

He cleared his throat as he turned back to Sadie. "Whatever I can do to help, you just let me know."

"Thank you. I do appreciate that." She offered a faint smile.

With those words, he backed out of the lot and headed to the hotel.

This was going to be his toughest investigation yet.

Sadie and Trevor arrived back at the hotel.

Kai would guard her door tonight while Trevor slept in the other room. They'd asked her permission to leave the door between the rooms open for security purposes.

She had agreed.

Sadie took a quick shower, craving some warm water to help her relax. Then she'd turned off the light beside her bed and crawled under the covers. Kai sat in a chair by the door. Apparently, he had gotten some rest earlier.

Knowing he was there made her feel better.

And Trevor . . . she frowned as his image filled her mind.

Could she trust him? Strange memories kept trying to materialize in her mind.

It was almost as if the two of them had known each other before her accident.

Sometimes it seemed as if Trevor cared about her as a person, not just as a job.

But if that were true, why would he lie to her?

Only one reason made sense—he had ulterior motives.

He knew something he wasn't telling her. But what?

She frowned as she sank farther into bed while a sick feeling roiled in her gut.

What if she'd been trusting the wrong person this

whole time? What if Guy was the one on her side and she'd chosen her ally incorrectly?

Her thoughts continued to race.

Should she confront Trevor? Demand he tell her the truth?

Something about that scenario didn't feel right.

Besides, if he *was* lying to her, he would only keep denying the truth. She'd only be showing her hand.

No, maybe keeping him close was a better idea.

Sadie needed to know what he knew. She had to be smart about this.

If she approached this situation correctly, maybe she could find the answers she needed.

That was her prayer as she tried to get some rest.

CHAPTER
TWENTY-SEVEN

TREVOR COULDN'T SLEEP. He'd known that would probably be the case. He had too much on his mind.

Once Sadie had been asleep for a while, he motioned for Kai to come into his room.

They stood beside the entry door, cracking it slightly so they could keep an eye on the hallway as they spoke.

This was just about as much privacy as they would get.

"What's going on?" Kai asked.

"I think Sadie remembered something." Trevor kept his voice low. "On the beach."

Kai's eyebrows shot up. "She wouldn't tell you what?"

"No. I didn't push too much. Didn't want it to seem suspicious."

Kai narrowed his eyes, his thoughts clearly churning as he put the pieces together. "What reason would she have for not telling you?"

"I'm not sure . . . unless it's something involving me." Trevor ran a hand over his face as he made the admission.

Kai's gaze lingered on him a moment longer.

His colleague could tell something was up. Trevor knew it wasn't fair to ask his friend to help while also keeping him in the dark. If he were in Kai's shoes, he'd want to know the truth—especially since their job required putting their lives on the line.

Trevor let out a long sigh. "The truth is that I was seeing Sadie before the accident. I just didn't tell Larchmont."

Kai's eyes lit with realization. "I knew it! I knew there was something more to this."

"I was supposed to meet her at the beach on the day she was hit, but I was running a few minutes late. I got there in time to see . . ." His voice cracked, and he couldn't finish his statement.

Kai continued to study Trevor's face. "You like her, don't you?"

"I *did* like her." Trevor shrugged before releasing a deep sigh. "Now I'm not sure about anything."

"It seems like a tangled web, doesn't it?"

Sadie's description earlier about the knotted yarn was perfect. Just when one knot had been unraveled, a new one formed. "Absolutely. Do you have any friends in WitSec?"

"I know of one guy."

"Could you talk to him? See if it's a possibility she's in the program?"

"I'll see what I can find out. In the meantime, what are you going to do?"

Trevor crossed his arms and glanced down the hallway again. It was still clear.

He looked back at Kai.

"I don't know," Trevor murmured with a frown. "I really don't know."

―――――

Sadie woke up with a start, her upper body springing forward as she gasped for air.

Something had jerked her from her sleep.

She glanced around.

The hotel room. That was right.

It was still dark in the room.

Not morning yet.

She slumped back down, trying to calm her racing heart. As far as she could remember, she hadn't even been having a bad dream.

But something had awoken her.

She looked at the door and saw Kai was gone.

Her heart rate intensified.

Where was he? Trevor had assured her his colleague would be there all night.

Had something happened to him? Or had he simply left her alone?

Then voices drifted from the other room.

Kai and Trevor. They were talking.

Relief swept through her—relief that quickly turned to curiosity.

Quietly, she climbed out of bed. Maybe she shouldn't eavesdrop. But she needed to know the truth. Until she knew who was being honest with her, she had no choice but to figure this out on her own.

She tiptoed toward the adjoining door, staying in the shadows.

The two men talked near the room entrance, keeping an eye on the hallway. She strained to make out what was being said.

"I think she remembered something," Trevor said. *"On the beach."*

"She wouldn't tell you what?"

"I didn't push too much. Didn't want it to seem suspicious."

"What reason would she have for not telling you?"

"I'm not sure . . . unless it's something involving me."

The rest of the conversation was garbled, and she couldn't make out their words.

But she knew enough.

Trevor was keeping something from her. Sadie's suspicions were correct. She wasn't losing her mind.

Part of her wanted to run. To forget about anything she'd brought with her, duck out the door into the hallway, and flee. To keep fleeing. To get away.

She couldn't do that.

Just as she'd decided earlier, she would stay close. Find out what Trevor knew. Figure out his true intentions.

For now.

But she wasn't ruling out the possibility of running later.

All she knew was that, even though she couldn't remember most of her background, she'd never been this terrified before in her life.

Nor had she ever felt so alone.

CHAPTER
TWENTY-EIGHT

TREVOR FINALLY FELL ASLEEP last night, even though he only got a few hours of shuteye. He had too many things on his mind.

Before 6:00 a.m., he got up, showered, and changed. Then he ran down to the lobby to grab breakfast for everyone. By the time he got back to the room, Sadie was awake and dressed and had the turned the TV on.

A new weariness lingered in her gaze as she looked up at him.

Normal, probably. But it still concerned him. Had something changed since last night? Had she remembered something? Why else would she seem so melancholy?

"Morning." He set a plastic tray with three cups

of coffee and some pastries on a small table in the corner.

"Morning." She turned the news off and rose from her reclined position on the bed.

Trevor glanced at Kai. "You want something to eat before you get some shuteye?"

His colleague shook his head. "I'll worry about that later. If you're good, I'm going to sleep for now. Try to get in two or three hours."

"Absolutely."

Kai disappeared into the other room and shut the door, leaving just Trevor and Sadie.

Trevor glanced at her again as she began to pick at a cream cheese pastry.

"I wasn't sure what you liked," he said.

That wasn't the truth. He knew she liked cream cheese pastries. He just couldn't let her know that.

"I'm not 100 percent sure what I like, other than that bacon cheeseburger I had last night." A faint smile brushed across her lips. "But this looks good. I just don't have much of an appetite."

"Understood." Trevor took another sip of his coffee. "How's your head today?"

She touched the back of it where she'd hit the concrete. "It's still sore."

"I can imagine."

She let out a long breath before abandoning the

pastry and pushing it away. "I need to find answers today, but I'm not sure how."

"Don't forget that you have a follow-up appointment with Dr. Conroy," Trevor reminded her.

"I had forgotten. Thanks." She paused. "Any updates on the office? Was the building a total loss?"

"As a matter of fact, they think part of the building can be salvaged. The fire mainly stayed at the back."

"That's good news."

"Yes, it is. As far as today is concerned, I had an idea." Trevor had been thinking everything through last night and this morning. "I think we should go back to your place and talk to some of your neighbors. I know the police have already done that. But maybe we'll catch someone else. Maybe they can fill you in on some details."

She nodded. "That sounds like a good idea. Let's do that."

"As soon as you finish eating, we will."

Sadie picked up her pastry and tossed it in the trash. "I'm ready to go now."

That familiar sense of dread filled Sadie as she and Trevor headed to her house.

That sense of wanting to know answers and also

fearing what those answers might mean clashed inside her.

She and Trevor pulled up to her house after a mostly quiet drive. She told herself she just needed to drink more coffee. But the truth was that she needed more time to think things through, especially after overhearing that conversation between Trevor and Kai last night.

"I think she remembered something," Trevor said. "On the beach."

"What reason would she have for not telling you?"

"I'm not sure . . . unless it's something involving me."

"You ready for this?" Trevor turned to her.

She shoved those thoughts aside, reminding herself not to trust Trevor too much, and shrugged. "I'm ready to find some answers."

She climbed out and turned to Trevor as he met her on the sidewalk. She glanced at her house. Saw the Bronco parked there.

Neither were familiar. She only knew it was her house and vehicle because she'd been told.

Had she had a happy life inside that house?

She swallowed hard and shifted her thoughts. "Where should we start?"

"What about over there?" He pointed to the house to the left of hers. "At least there's a car in the driveway."

"Sounds like a plan."

They headed toward the house, and Trevor knocked on the door.

Sadie didn't know exactly what she would say if someone answered. But she hoped it would make sense.

A few minutes later, a woman in her mid-sixties answered. She had blonde hair to her chin, a thin build, and wore neat capris with a white top.

Her eyes instantly lit with recognition. "Sadie . . . I heard what happened to you. I'm so sorry."

Sadie swallowed hard. "Thanks. I don't know if you heard that I lost my memory."

"What?" Her voice turned wispy with surprise.

"It's true. I'm still trying to put together a few things, and I hoped you might be able to help."

"I can imagine." The woman pressed a hand against her chest. "I'm Victoria, by the way."

"Hi, Victoria. This is my . . . friend, Trevor. He's helping me through some of this. Do you mind if we ask you a few questions about . . . well, about me?"

"Not at all." She opened the door wider. "Why don't you come inside and sit down?"

They walked into her small living room and took seats on a cream-colored couch.

Sadie wasted no time diving into her questions. "What can you tell me about having me as a neighbor?"

Victoria's eyebrows slowly rose as she seemed to

think through her words. "You've always been very pleasant. Kind of quiet, and you keep to yourself for the most part. But you're always friendly when I see you. You always ask how I'm doing, and you've helped me bring in my groceries a couple of times."

At least Sadie liked that image of herself.

"Anything else you can think of?" she asked.

"Not really." Victoria shrugged. "I mean, I personally found your late-night meetings to be strange."

"My late-night meetings?"

"I'm a bit of an insomniac. But, yes, quite often you have someone stop by at random hours of the night, almost like it's a normal thing. Then you leave in the morning for work as if nothing happened."

Sadie blinked. "How many nights a week do I have these meetings?"

"It varies. Probably a couple of times."

"The same person each time?" she asked.

"I'm pretty sure it's the same car. I haven't really seen who gets out, though. It's always dark, and whoever you meet with wears dark colors."

"How long does this person usually stay?" Trevor asked.

Victoria blew out a breath. "Not long. Maybe ten or fifteen minutes. That makes it seem even stranger."

"You can say that again . . ." Sadie muttered.

CHAPTER
TWENTY-NINE

TREVOR LISTENED CAREFULLY.

Late-night visits? Who was coming to her place in the middle of the night and only staying for ten or fifteen minutes?

It was another question they needed to get to the bottom of.

"Did you tell the police that?" Trevor asked.

"No, I didn't think it was important." She paused. "Should I?"

"It's probably not a big deal." Trevor wanted to investigate first before the police found out.

They thanked Victoria, and she walked them to the door. But before she closed it, she said, "You should talk to Melanie across the street."

"Why is that?" Sadie asked.

"Because out of everyone who lives on this street, you talk to her the most."

"Is that right?" Sadie said. "Thank you for that. Do you know if she's home now?"

"She's a stay-at-home mom with two kids who aren't in school yet. I'd say there's a good chance she is."

"Thank you again," Sadie muttered.

Without talking about it, Sadie and Trevor headed across the street to Melanie's house.

Before they even reached the door, it opened.

A woman near Sadie's age stood there, a toddler on her hip.

"Sadie . . . am I ever glad to see you!" Melanie—Trevor could only assume that was who the woman was—reached for Sadie and pulled her into a hug.

Some grape jelly on her toddler's cheek stuck to Sadie's shirt when she stepped back, but Sadie didn't seem to mind. If she noticed, she ignored it.

"I've been hoping you'd stop by." Melanie tilted her head as her voice dropped with compassion. "We've all been so worried."

Sadie shifted awkwardly in front of her neighbor. "You know I've lost most of my memories, right?"

Most of her memories? Trevor mused. He thought Sadie had lost *all* her memories.

Maybe it had been a misspeak.

They walked into the living room, where Melanie

put her toddler on the floor behind a baby gate. The boy began running around with his little sister. The whole place was a kiddie wonderland with a plastic slide, colorful toys, and stuffed animals everywhere.

Before Trevor could dive into any questions, Melanie turned toward him. "Are you the new guy?"

Trevor's back tightened. "The new guy?"

"What do you mean?" A new eagerness filled Sadie's voice.

Melanie turned back to Sadie. "The last time we spoke, you said you'd met some new guy. Someone you really liked. You seemed happy."

Trevor could hardly breathe. Was Melanie referring to him? He didn't want to jump to any conclusions.

But if Melanie *was* referring to him, it brought him a surprising measure of happiness.

Then Trevor reminded himself to stay in check.

There were still too many uncertainties.

In fact, maybe this man Sadie was meeting in the middle of the night was her new love interest. Or maybe he was Guy.

Or maybe he was . . . one of Trevor's enemies she was slipping information to.

His jaw tightened.

He didn't like any of those possibilities.

"I told you I'd just met somebody?" Could Sadie have been referring to Guy? "Did I say anything else?"

"You were all hush-hush about it," Melanie said. "But you looked really excited, and I was happy for you."

"Did I tell you anything else about him?" Sadie asked.

Melanie shook her head. "No, not really. I'm sorry. I wish I could be more help. But I think you were waiting to see how things worked out before you told me very many details." Melanie's gaze went to Trevor. "Speaking of which, you never told me who this is."

Sadie stumbled to find the right words. How did she describe Trevor? Her bodyguard?

That would raise some questions.

A friend?

That didn't ring true either.

"I'm working private security for her," Trevor answered for her. "Considering the fact someone tried to kill her, it seemed in her best interest."

Melanie took a step back as if suddenly second-guessing her choice to let them into the house. "I see."

"I won't take up much more of your time." Sadie seemed to sense her friend's sudden fear. "But is there anything else I may have told you that might help me remember? Anyone else I can talk to? I've already been in to work, and I talked to Victoria across the street."

Melanie pressed her lips together before frowning and shaking her head. "Not that I know of. You seemed pretty content just working and doing your own thing. You're not the type who needs to be out all the time being social. Not that you're a hermit or anything. You're a nice in-between, you know?"

Sadie didn't mind that description of herself. It seemed to fit the person she sensed she'd been. "You said I've only lived here six months? Do you know where I moved from?"

Melanie shook her head. "No, you never mentioned it. I mean, I just assumed you'd probably lived in an apartment and had saved up money to buy a house."

Sadie nodded. "That would make sense."

Melanie tilted her head to the side, clearly trying to wrap up the conversation. "It's so good to see you, Sadie. I hope you get your memories back. I'd love to hang out sometime once all this passes over."

Sadie smiled, trying to push away all the heaviness she felt. "I would love that too."

But what if this never passed? What if this was her new normal?

CHAPTER
THIRTY

"I WANT to go to the beach," Sadie announced she climbed back into Trevor's truck.

He turned to her, unable to conceal his surprise. "What was that?"

"I know it might seem rash, but I just need to clear my head. That's the only place I can think to go to do that."

"Sure. We can go to the beach. The same one as yesterday?"

"Whichever one is closest."

He put his truck in Drive and took off down the road. The nearest beach wasn't far, and it was a larger access than the one where he and Sadie normally met.

He drove five minutes down the road before pulling into the lot. A few other vehicles were already there, which wasn't surprising since it was summertime.

They climbed out, but instead of walking toward the beach, she paused. "I just need to run to the restroom a moment, if you don't mind."

"Not at all."

As Sadie disappeared inside the bathroom, Trevor waited outside. He remained on guard just in case anyone suspicious appeared.

A footstep sounded behind him, and he turned, ready to defend himself—and Sadie.

He dropped his arms when he spotted Larchmont standing there wearing khaki shorts and a blue T-shirt—a very un-Larchmont-like outfit. He wouldn't fit in here in his usual professional clothing, however.

"Where did you come from?" Trevor glanced around, looking for his boss's car.

It wasn't in sight.

"That's not important." Larchmont's eyes were obscured by his sunglasses, a fact that matched his aloof tone. "I've been trying to catch you alone."

"Well, you succeeded. Here I am. However, I don't know when Sadie is going to be out. We shouldn't be seen together."

"This is important," Larchmont said. "Otherwise, I wouldn't be here. That man who died—"

"I know. He was seen arguing with Sadie."

"He worked for Frederick Moreau."

"What?" Trevor's voice lilted higher.

"I don't know who she's working for, but I wouldn't trust anything she says."

Sadie wasn't sneaky.

At least, to the best of her knowledge she wasn't sneaky.

But as she'd started to leave the restroom, she paused.

Two men were chatting outside.

One of them was Trevor, but she wasn't sure who the other man was. She didn't recognize the voice.

Her curiosity got the best of her, and she slipped back inside the restroom.

She went to one of the toilets and stood on top of the seat. A small window stretched above the stall. She peered out of it, determined to see the mystery man Trevor was talking to.

A man with a shock of white hair stood there, speaking in quiet tones to Trevor.

When Sadie saw him, a flash of something hit her, and she nearly fell off the toilet.

She'd seen that man before. But where? When?

In the photos, she realized. The ones she had on the file on her computer in the office.

Then memories began pummeling her.

Memories of following the man. Seeing him meeting with someone.

Someone dangerous.

Seeing him exchange something with that very man.

Sadie couldn't remember all the details. Had no idea who the man was. What had been exchanged. Who the man was he'd been meeting with.

She only knew he was trouble.

But if Trevor was talking to this man right now . . .

She shook her head, blinking several times trying to clear her thoughts.

She didn't want to believe Trevor was a bad guy. But she couldn't deny the facts—not if she was smart.

None of this made sense.

Her thoughts churned.

"He worked for Frederick Moreau," the stranger said.

Frederick Moreau? Who was Frederick Moreau?

"Getting to know her may not work," the stranger said. "We may have to use more extreme measures."

Then silence stretched.

Someone murmured something indecipherable.

Was it Trevor? What was he saying? Was he agreeing? Whispering a plan to take her out?

"You okay in there?" Trevor suddenly yelled toward the bathroom.

Sadie jumped. Her heart pounded so hard into her chest that it nearly ached. "I'm fine. I'll just be a few more minutes."

She climbed from the toilet and grabbed her phone.

She did a search for Trevor McGrath, something she probably should have done earlier.

She scanned the results on the screen.

There weren't many.

She kept looking, but the search for information on Trevor hadn't led to much, almost like . . . he didn't exist.

Much like her.

Nausea swirled in her gut.

What kind of trouble had she gotten herself into?

CHAPTER
THIRTY-ONE

SADIE'S BLOOD WENT COLD.

Staying around Trevor had been one of the worst decisions she could have made.

She'd been wrong. She didn't need to keep him close.

She needed to get far away.

Her heart pounding in her ears, she tried to think through a plan. If she stuck around much longer, he might kill her. She might be out of time—especially if that man Trevor was meeting with was as dangerous as her gut told her he was.

Trevor still talked to the stranger outside.

She only had minutes to act.

Quietly, she slipped her phone back into her pocket. Then she crept from the stall toward the bathroom door.

She cracked it open.

The door didn't make a sound.

She stepped outside. Let the door close behind her.

Still no sounds.

She peered toward where Trevor now stood. He couldn't see her. He was still talking to that man. Still distracted.

Wasting no more time, she hurried to the opposite side of the building.

Then she took off in a desperate run across the parking lot toward the tree-lined street in the distance.

Trevor sighed, ready for a break from this conversation with Larchmont.

What was taking Sadie so long?

He didn't want to rush her. But she really had been in the bathroom a long time.

He turned away from Larchmont and toward the bathroom window. "Sadie?"

This time, there was no answer.

Tension crept up his spine.

He and Larchmont exchanged a look.

Trevor peered around the corner in time to see Sadie darting across the parking lot.

Had she overheard part of his conversation with Larchmont?

Or had her memories returned?

Trevor took off after her. "Sadie!"

She didn't look back at him.

Instead, she charged full speed ahead, fleeing as if her life depended on it.

He had to catch her. To explain. To make things right.

Just as that thought filled his mind, a car squealed into the parking lot.

Flashbacks of Sadie being hit filled him.

Not again. *Please, Lord, not again . . .*

"Look out!" he called.

Instead, the driver slammed on brakes. A man in black jumped from the vehicle. Grabbed Sadie. Threw her into the back seat.

No! Trevor bolted toward the car.

But before he could stop them, the car peeled out of the parking lot.

With Sadie inside.

CHAPTER
THIRTY-TWO

PANIC SURGED THROUGH SADIE.

What had just happened?

A man pressed his hand over her mouth and clutched her arms against her using his other arm. She fought with everything she had in her, desperate to escape his hold.

She wasn't going to let him get away with this unscathed.

But the man was so much stronger than she was.

Sadie lifted her foot, preparing to ram it into the man's shin.

Then she heard a click followed by, "I wouldn't do that if I were you."

The man had a gun, she realized.

Sadie froze.

Maybe running from Trevor had been a bad idea. She'd fled one danger and ran right into another.

Two men were in the car, the one holding her hostage in the back seat and the one driving.

She couldn't see the man gripping her, but she glanced at the driver. He wore a black cap, and she couldn't make out many details about him other than the fact he was blond.

And the fact he was a terrible driver.

He sped away, driving erratically down the street and nearly sideswiping another vehicle.

What did these guys plan on doing with her?

Would she recognize them if she got a good look at their faces? If her memories were restored?

It didn't matter. All she knew was that they were dangerous.

"The road is blocked up ahead," the man beside her said. "They're repaving it. There's a detour."

She glanced out the front windshield.

Saw the barricade in the road.

Then she heard a vehicle gunning it behind them.

She turned and saw Trevor's truck.

She wanted to believe he was coming to help. But she didn't know what to believe anymore.

The driver slowed. "What should I do?"

"Bust through it," the man beside her suggested.

"Are you crazy? I can't do that!"

The two men began to argue, seeming to forget about Sadie a minute.

This was her opportunity.

Most likely her *only* opportunity.

If she screwed this up, she might die.

But if she didn't try anything, she would die.

She had no doubt about that.

She needed to take her chances.

As her captor barked something to the driver, she jammed her foot into the door handle.

The door flew open.

With no time to waste, Sadie sprang forward.

Her sudden move took the man by surprise. His grip remained loosened.

She prayed he didn't pull the trigger.

Before he could fully realize what was going on, she jumped from the car and rolled into a ditch.

Brakes screeched, and she braced herself, knowing this wasn't over yet.

As she pressed her eyes closed, her mind seemed to blip, and memories—or something like a memory—filled her.

"There!" Trevor pointed to the road ahead.

Thankfully, Larchmont had seen what was going on. He had jumped into Trevor's truck—Trevor had left the keys inside—and picked him up. Then they'd taken off after the sedan.

Ahead, the road was barricaded, and construction cones had been set up.

The car was slowing down.

What were these guys going to do?

Then the back door flew open.

Sadie rolled on the ground like a ragdoll and landed in a ditch.

Larchmont threw on brakes.

Trevor started to get out. But he wasn't sure what these guys were planning.

The next instant, the sedan made a U-turn and sped past them in the opposite direction. The dark windows obscured the people inside.

He would tell Larchmont to follow it. But he had to check on Sadie. Had to know she was okay.

Though it appeared she'd jumped out of the car, she could have been pushed.

Or worse . . . they could have done something to her and then shoved her dead body out.

Trevor's heart lurched into his throat at the thought.

As the other car raced in the opposite direction, he launched out of the truck and ran toward Sadie.

As soon as he reached her, she moaned and turned over in the grass.

She was alive!

He thanked God for that.

"Sadie, are you okay?" He knelt on the ground beside her.

She sat up and squinted. Before responding, she glanced at the road. Saw the other car had disappeared.

Her shoulders relaxed as she said, "Yeah, I think so."

Trevor helped her to her feet, and she brushed the grass from her clothing. Then she glanced around again, her gaze stopping on his truck.

How was he going to explain Larchmont?

But as he followed her gaze, he realized Larchmont was nowhere to be seen.

Where had he gone?

His boss had always been able to vanish like a ghost.

There was no sign he'd ever been there.

"Let's get you to the truck so you can sit down," Trevor said.

He kept an arm around Sadie as he led her to the passenger side and helped her into the seat.

He had so many questions for her.

Where did he even start?

CHAPTER
THIRTY-THREE

TREVOR DROVE FARTHER DOWN the road, away from what had just happened. Then he veered off onto a gravel pullover and threw his truck in Park.

He licked his lips before he turned toward Sadie. "Why did you run?"

"I overheard the conversation you were having with that man." Sadie narrowed her eyes. She didn't look scared.

She looked mad. Furious, actually.

"I heard him say, 'Getting to know her may not work. We may have to use more extreme measures.'"

His eyebrows flung up. He could only imagine the conclusions she'd drawn. "It's not what you think."

Her gaze cut to his. "It's not? Because I'm not sure you have any clue what I'm thinking right now."

Her tone made it clear she was not happy.

Trevor needed to do some major damage control before she walked out of his life, never to return. "What are you thinking?"

With an exasperated sigh, she opened the passenger side door and hurried out.

Trevor scrambled out after her. Thankfully, she paused in front of the truck, probably just needing some fresh air.

A flash of irritation ripped through her gaze as she turned to him. "You want to know what I'm thinking? I'm thinking you've been lying to me this whole time. I think you knew me before all this happened. I even have to wonder if you're behind all this." She shook her head. "But it doesn't make sense. If you're behind this, then why did those other guys grab me?"

"I'm not behind what happened to you." Trevor knew he couldn't keep this to himself anymore. If he tried, Sadie would only run again. Instead, he swallowed hard before asking, "You want the truth?"

"I would *love* the truth."

He hauled in a deep breath, hoping he didn't regret this. "The truth is, you and I went on a few dates before you lost your memory. I was heading to the beach to meet you when I saw the car ram into you."

Her eyes widened. "If that's true, why didn't you tell me?"

His jaw twitched. "I was advised not to."

She shook her head. "Please, explain more. Because I'm very confused."

"I *do* work for a private security agency, and much of what we do is classified. That means there are a lot of protocols we go through in our personal lives as well, including who we date."

"Keep going."

"I skipped over those protocols when I met you," Trevor continued. "I guess I felt like being a rebel and not sticking to the rules. After the accident, my boss heard what happened and did a background check on you. He discovered you don't really exist."

Sadie blinked and rapidly shook her head. "What does that even mean? Of *course* I exist. Here I am."

"Yes, in reality you exist. But your background . . . it's been fabricated."

Her eyes widened as shockwaves seemed to wash over her. "If that's true, then who am I?"

———

Sadie didn't want to believe Trevor. She wanted to think he wasn't telling the truth. That, despite his soft tones, he was making all this up just to confuse her more.

But he sounded so sincere.

However, she still had more questions before she drew any conclusions.

"The man you were talking to outside the bathroom?" she continued. "He's the one who was in those photos on my computer."

"That's what I was afraid of. I had my suspicions . . ."

"Is he your boss?"

"He is," Trevor said. "His name is Larchmont, and he's a bit of an apparition. He pops up when you least expect it. Then he's gone just as fast."

"Is there any reason I should have known him?"

"None that I can think of."

Sadie nodded slowly as she listened, taking everything with a grain of salt. "When you say I don't have a past, how do you explain that?"

"That's what I'm trying to figure out. Larchmont thought I should stay close to you. Thought maybe you had ulterior motives for going on those dates with me, motives that might involve the organization I work for. He wanted me to find out if that was accurate, and he thought the best way to do that was by not admitting we had a past relationship."

"And if I regained my memories?"

"Then I would have to deal with that when the time came."

Sadie studied Trevor another moment. A haunted look floated in his eyes almost as if he didn't approve of his boss's instructions. Like he'd had a crisis of conscience.

But that still didn't explain Sadie's lack of a background. How was that even possible?

Nothing made sense.

"I'm sorry, Sadie." Trevor's voice dipped low with remorse. "I never meant for any of this to happen. I just thought I'd met a great girl I wanted to see again and again and again. Then everything unfolded, and I was swept up in this crazy, confusing whirlwind. I'm not trying to make excuses, but I *am* trying to explain myself and how I came to be put in this position."

He sounded sincere, and Sadie wanted to believe him. But she also wanted to be angry with him. She wanted to pick apart everything he'd said to find any morsel of deceit.

Instead, she said, "I get it. Maybe. I mean, I don't really know what to think anymore. Why wouldn't I have a documented history? Medical records. School transcripts. Something tangible. Anything."

"Usually, people have blank spaces in their past because they're hiding something," he said. "Witness protection maybe?"

She let that thought settle for a moment, wondering if there was any merit to it. At this point, anything was a possibility, she supposed.

"Did your boss talk to the US Marshals?" Again, a random fact she recalled while she remembered no aspects of her actual life. "Don't they handle cases like that?"

"They do." Trevor's gaze remained serious, almost burdened. "Kai has a contact in that agency, but he couldn't find any record you were a part of their program. However, that information is highly classified, so they might not have been forthcoming."

"So what are the other possibilities?"

Trevor rubbed his neck as if he didn't want to say what he had to say next. "The other possibility is maybe you work for one of my enemies, and you came to find out information to destroy me . . . and maybe you made some of your own enemies in the process."

CHAPTER
THIRTY-FOUR

TREVOR WATCHED SADIE'S FACE.

She didn't like that last statement.

She didn't see herself as someone who could be a bad guy—which was a good thing.

Trevor didn't want to believe that either. But he had to face the truth. Trying to skirt around reality wouldn't do him any good. In fact, it could end up getting him killed.

He turned back to her, ready to tell her more. "The truth is, we believe you have an affiliation with Frederick Moreau."

"Who is Frederick Moreau?" She blinked in confusion.

"He's a bad person, to put it lightly. Involved in human trafficking, arms dealing, and a host of other illegal and dangerous activities."

"And why would you believe I'm affiliated with him?"

"You were seen meeting with one of his guys. Frederick himself is in prison, but he still has plenty of minions out there willing to do his bidding. He's not very happy with me, to say the least. I'm the one who helped bring him down. Maybe you work for him."

Sadie stared at him, disbelief in her eyes. It was a lot to process. He knew that.

And it sounded far-fetched. Except, in his world, it wasn't.

Maybe not in Sadie's world either.

"Why would I work for a man like that?" she finally asked.

"There's a chance you were sent to find out information on me for what could ultimately lead to my downfall. Then the hit-and-run happened before you could complete your mission. I'm still not sure who's responsible for that, however. Or why. There are lots of questions."

She shook her head, rubbing the skin between her eyes. "I would never betray someone like that."

His heart softened a moment. "I would like to believe that also. But with your memory loss . . . anything is possible."

"Even with my memory loss, don't you think I'd know deep down if I'm capable of that? I feel like I still know who I am on the inside even if I don't remember all the details of my life."

"I don't know what to tell you." Trevor searched for the right words to say, but there were none for a situation like this. There had been too many lies. Too much deceit.

Too much evil.

They stood there in silence a moment, tension crackling between them.

Finally, Sadie looked back at him. "You said the two of us went on several dates? So you *did* know me."

His jaw tightened at the memories, at the subtle hurt in her voice. "I always try to remain carefully guarded. Now, the first time I actually let down my guard, it was a major mistake. It won't happen again."

Something flashed in her eyes. Was that regret? Disappointment? Maybe even hurt.

Trevor was probably just seeing what he wanted to see.

What he and Sadie had between them wasn't real, and the sooner he came to terms with that, the better.

Sadie's thoughts continued to race through everything she'd just learned.

She couldn't believe Trevor had known all this and not shared it with her.

Then again, if she truly was working for a crime lord, she supposed she understood why he hadn't.

Everything inside her told her that she wouldn't intentionally hurt anyone.

But how was she to know what was true and what wasn't true? Could her gut feelings really be trusted? She'd like to think so. But any sense of balance she'd begun to feel had been turned upside down.

Then there were those flashes of memory that had hit her when she had jumped out of that car.

Memories of meeting with a stranger in the woods. Whispering to him.

Seeing him get upset.

Then he'd pushed her.

She'd pushed him back.

Then his face came into view.

It was the dead man, the one who'd died only hours before she'd been hit by that car.

She glanced back up at Trevor. "Did I kill that man?"

Trevor hesitated before shrugging. "If you asked me a day ago, I would have said no. But right now, I have to admit I have no idea. You were living a double life. Having meetings in the middle of the night. Associated with a crime boss. Yet, by day you worked for an elevator company and were dating Guy Merchant. Nothing really makes sense to me right now either."

Sadie heard the pain in his voice and wished she could take it away. But she couldn't. That hurt might very well be for a good reason.

What if she wasn't the person she'd assumed she was? What if she'd killed that man who had been found dead near town? Then what if someone she was working for had tried to kill her to cover it all up?

It all seemed so far-fetched.

But this was the reality of her life right now. She needed to figure out how she would proceed.

Before they could talk any longer, a car pulled up and parked behind them.

Trevor reached for his gun as he turned to the vehicle, clearly bracing for a fight.

CHAPTER
THIRTY-FIVE

TREVOR BRISTLED as he watched Guy stalk toward them. Based on the veins popping out at Guy's temples, he wasn't very happy.

The man paused in front of them, his hands fisted at his side.

Despite everything that happened between Trevor and Sadie, he still found himself nudging his way in front of her as a protective measure.

"I happened to be driving past and saw you guys standing out here," he muttered with a half eye roll. "How fortuitous."

"What do you want, Guy?" Trevor asked.

"I want you to stop hanging out with my girlfriend." Guy sneered as he said the words. "She's never going to remember *me* if she's always with *you*."

"That's not your choice," Trevor said. "I'm not forcing her to hang out with me. In fact, she hired me to keep her safe. I'm only doing my job."

"There's something about you I don't like." Guy jabbed his finger into Trevor's chest.

Trevor's muscles tightened even more. "You don't want to do that."

"Maybe I do."

"You two!" Sadie's voice cut through the tension of the moment. "I'm perfectly capable of speaking for myself."

They both turned toward her.

She turned toward Guy first. "Everything Trevor said is correct. He's simply someone I hired, and that's it."

Trevor flushed. Maybe Sadie had said those words on purpose, wanting to put him in his place. He couldn't blame her for that, but he had to admit her statement still hurt.

"Until I can figure out what's going on in my life, I'm keeping my distance from everybody. That includes you two. Things aren't adding up." She crossed her arms and looked back at Guy again. "Maybe *you* can tell me why."

Guy's eyes narrowed. "What do you mean by that?"

"I mean, there were things going on in my life that I'm not comfortable with, and I'm trying to get to the bottom of it. Is there anything you can tell me about my life that might help me? And be honest. I'll eventually find out if you're lying to me."

A puzzled look crossed his face, and he shook his head. "I don't know anything important. I just know we enjoyed going to dinner together."

"Just dinner?" Sadie asked.

Trevor listened carefully, curious as to where this was going.

"Well, yeah. Dinner." Guy shrugged.

Sadie's eyes narrowed. "Were we really even dating?"

"I mean, we went out several times." An edge of hurt crept into his voice.

"But we weren't serious, were we?"

He ran a hand over his face. "Depends on what you mean by *serious*."

A better picture formed in Trevor's mind as he let Sadie do the talking.

He hadn't liked this guy from the start. Now he knew why.

"You wanted us to be more serious, and when you heard about my accident you decided to move in," Sadie said. "Then when you found out I didn't have my memories, you decided to plant the idea in my head that we were a couple. I'm not denying that we may have gone out to eat, but our relationship is not what you're presenting it to be. We were friends."

"It's not like that. Not really." Guy frowned and let out a long breath.

"Then what is it like? Really?"

"I like you. If all this hadn't happened, I think we would have moved forward into something more serious and committed."

She shook her head and let out a sardonic chuckle. "You were trying to take advantage of me after my accident. That's despicable."

He raked a hand through his hair, the tension inside him clearly mounting with each tidbit of truth that emerged.

"It's not like that," he repeated again.

Sadie stepped closer. "What else can you tell me? Did I do anything suspicious in the week before my accident?"

"You were just asking a lot of questions about the company," he said. "How it operated. Who did what. I wondered if some of your number crunching wasn't adding up."

"Did I say that?" Sadie asked.

He shook his head. "I was reading between the lines."

"Did you tell her anything?" Trevor asked. "Anything that caught her interest?"

"I don't think so. She almost looked disappointed. But there were a million other things I wanted to talk about—like the two of us and our future together."

Trevor was tired of listening to this guy talk. He stepped closer.

"It's time for you to get to your doctor's appointment," he reminded Sadie.

Visible relief washed over her features. "Okay then. I've got to go. I'll see you around, Guy. Please don't confront me anymore about this."

With those words, they climbed back into Trevor's truck and took off for the hospital.

Sadie's thoughts raced.

Thank goodness, she'd put everything together. There had just been something about that whole situation with Guy that hadn't rung true with her.

Now she knew.

Guy *wanted* there to be something more between them than what was actually present. The fact he'd lied to her in order to work out things to his advantage only upset her more.

The thing was, Guy didn't even seem like her type. So why had she gone out on several dates with him?

She wasn't sure exactly how to put everything together.

As Trevor glanced at her from the driver's seat,

her wrath toward Guy suddenly turned back onto Trevor.

Trevor hadn't been much better. He'd also been deceiving her about their past relationship. Guy, she had expected it from. Trevor . . . she'd thought she could trust him.

However, it also appeared that Sadie had been deceiving a lot of people as well.

Nothing made sense right now. Sadie couldn't be self-righteous when she was doing the same things as those she was upset with.

But she would like to think she had a better reason for it. Would like to think she hadn't been working for a crime boss.

She remained quiet for the rest of the ride, staring out the window until they reached the hospital.

As they walked inside, memories of when Sadie had last been here filled her mind. She'd felt so uncertain. So confused. So hopeless, really.

It had only been a couple of days and, honestly, things still didn't make much sense.

She needed her memories back. She wished there was something she could do to accelerate this whole process. But it wasn't that easy.

They headed up the elevator to the third floor, and Sadie braced herself for her meeting with Dr. Conroy, praying for a positive report.

CHAPTER
THIRTY-SIX

TREVOR WAITED ANXIOUSLY outside the room while Sadie met with the doctor.

She hadn't invited him in, and he understood why. A person's medical health was a private matter. He respected that.

But Trevor hoped for her sake she'd gotten some good news.

Everything was quickly unraveling. Before too long, any semblance of peace would end up as a pile of discarded scraps.

Finally, she stepped out of the exam room, her eyes brighter than earlier.

She paused near him. "Dr. Conroy says I'm progressing as I should be. No other symptoms have popped up, so that's good."

Trevor rose and nodded, hating this new tension

between them. "I'm glad to hear that. I know you could use some good news."

"You can say that again." She let out a feeble breath of air, almost as if attempting a laugh but failing. "I'm ready to get out of here. Maybe we can grab a bite to eat. I don't know about you, but I'm hungry."

He'd halfway expected Sadie to fire him. With all the deceit between them, it wouldn't surprise him.

But she didn't say anything regarding that.

He still needed to keep her close for now, so he saw the food idea as a win.

"Let's go," he murmured.

They walked back to the elevator, awkward silence falling between them as they waited for the doors to open.

For a moment, Trevor wondered what might have developed between them if all the lies didn't exist.

He couldn't see himself ever meeting someone like Sadie—the Sadie he knew, at least—again. Even if he did, he wasn't sure he'd ever be willing to open himself up to someone else, not after this catastrophe.

Maybe it was better if he did exactly what Larchmont had told him. To simply find contentment in being single and being married to his job.

Things were a lot less complicated that way.

The elevator dinged, and they stepped inside. They had the car to themselves.

He pressed the button for the first floor and watched as the doors slowly began to close.

Then a hand slipped between the doors and stopped them from closing.

A man rushed inside. "Sorry about that!"

Except this guy didn't exactly look like a hospital employee, Trevor mused. Not even a visitor.

No, an aura of danger surrounded him.

Instead of turning to face the doors, the man paused in front of them.

Facing them.

As the door closed behind the man, Trevor's breath caught.

This was the man who'd been watching him and Sadie earlier. The one who'd been in the hospital right after Sadie was first admitted. The one Trevor had chased. The one he'd seen at the restaurant, if he had to guess.

He was here.

In the elevator.

With them.

Trevor braced himself for the fight of his life and reached for his gun.

"You don't need to draw that," the man muttered

before moving his sweatshirt aside. "I have one too. This will be a lot easier if we just use words."

Sadie sucked in a breath as she watched the man.

He was the man she'd seen outside the hospital.

The one who had made her panic surge.

Now he was here. With them.

Trevor lowered his hand, but his arm looked triggered, as if at the first sign of danger, he would draw his weapon.

Instead, Trevor stepped forward until he stood between her and this stranger. "What do you want?"

"Just to talk."

"Who are you and why have you been following us?" Trevor demanded.

The man reached over and pressed the Emergency Stop button. The elevator lurched to a halt, and a bell began to ring, the screeching loud and overwhelming.

Sadie's pulse beat harder, pounding in her chest with ferocity. What exactly was this guy planning?

"I'm not here to hurt you," the guy said over the sound of the alarm.

"Then why are you here?" Trevor asked.

"We need to talk. But not here. Somewhere private. Every time I try to get close to talk to you, someone interrupts my plans."

"How do I know you're not setting us up?" Trevor asked.

"You don't," the man said. "You're just going to have to trust me."

Trusting strangers wasn't something that seemed prudent at the moment.

"Meet me at Clinch Park in two hours, and I'll explain everything then."

He let go of the alarm button, and the screeching bell turned off. The elevator continued down then the doors opened.

Just as quickly as he'd appeared, the man was gone.

Sadie sucked in a deep breath, trying to process what had just happened. Finally, she asked, "What was that about?"

Trevor shook his head, his gaze hard. "I have no idea."

"You know that guy could have killed us right in the elevator if he'd wanted to." She gave Trevor a second glance. "I mean, you could have stopped him, but you know what I'm getting at. You think this guy really might be a good guy?"

He shrugged. "At this point, I have no idea what to think."

"So you want to meet him?"

Trevor let out a long, drawn-out breath. "I don't think we have much choice."

CHAPTER
THIRTY-SEVEN

TREVOR AND SADIE decided to grab something to eat at a Mexican restaurant down the road.

They remained quiet on the drive.

Trevor couldn't stop thinking about that man and who he might be.

He didn't recognize the guy—other than as the man who'd been following them. Did he work for Frederick Moreau?

It seemed like a good possibility.

Trevor didn't expect Sadie to know anything more than he did so he didn't ask any questions.

But as they headed down the street, he glanced in his rearview mirror and saw a car tailing them. "Oh, great . . ."

"What is it?" Sadie's voice stretched thin with anxiety.

He stared at the dark-colored sedan. "I think we're being followed."

"By the guy from the elevator?" She swung her head back to look at the road behind them.

"It's hard to say."

It was hard to know who any of their enemies were. In fact, Trevor could be sitting beside an enemy right now. It was impossible to know for sure.

For the moment, he simply needed to concentrate on getting away from this guy alive.

Trevor took a sharp right turn.

Sadie gasped beside him and reached for the grab bar overhead.

He glanced in the rearview mirror. The sedan was still there.

"Why do you think they're following us?" Sadie's voice trembled as she asked the question.

"You probably don't want to know." His grip on the steering wheel tightened.

There was no good reason for the car to follow them. Only if that driver wanted to harm them. If someone thought Sadie was getting too close to the truth, that could very well be the case.

He took another turn, this time to the left. Several cars threw on their brakes as he raced across an intersection.

Trevor prayed this might work.

But as he heard more vehicles laying on their horns, he knew that wasn't the case.

That car was still behind him, the driver becoming more aggressive by the moment.

"What are we going to do?" Sadie sounded breathless.

"Right now, I'm just trying to lose them."

"And if that's not possible?"

His throat tightened at her question and, before he could answer, a new sound split the air.

Two sounds, almost simultaneous.

Gunfire and glass shattering.

His back window exploded into a million pieces as he shouted, "Get down!"

Sadie's heart pounded into her ears so loudly she could hardly hear anything else.

These guys meant serious business. No more hiding in the shadows or doing things in secret.

They were going all out in their attempts to silence either Trevor or Sadie. Or both.

Terror rippled through her.

Trevor jerked the steering wheel again, and Sadie slammed into the door.

"Trevor?" Desperation crackled in her voice. But

she didn't dare lift her head to see what was going on.

"I'm doing my best here . . ."

"I know you are."

Then the windshield shattered, raining glass all over her. A muffled scream escaped before she could stop it.

Those guys—there had to be at least two, one driving, the other shooting—were still firing. Scaring them wasn't enough.

These men were out for blood.

How would she and Trevor get out of this?

More horns honked around them. She had a feeling Trevor was trying to get out of town so no one else would be in danger.

Then she heard the sirens.

The police had been notified.

Maybe the cops would scare these guys, and they'd back off.

Then again, they were no holds barred right now.

It seemed as if they'd been given a mission to kill, whatever the cost.

What if Trevor died as a result?

Did this all go back to her? Or did some of this have to do with Trevor?

She wished she had some answers.

Maybe that man they'd met in the elevator knew something. Maybe he could explain some things.

Another bullet cut through the air, the sound causing her muscles to jerk.

Trevor muttered something under his breath.

They couldn't keep going like this. Eventually, something would stop them. An empty fuel tank. An accident. A fatal gunshot.

Something!

Trevor sucked in a breath.

Sadie didn't like the sound of that.

"Trevor?" she called over the roar of the wind coming in through the broken windshield.

"Hold on," he ordered.

Part of her didn't want to know what that meant.

CHAPTER
THIRTY-EIGHT

TREVOR SPOTTED the road work ahead, and he had to make a quick decision.

He knew part of the roadway had washed out in a recent flood. At this time of the day, the workers should be gone.

He was going to take a chance.

He pressed on the accelerator and blew through the barriers set out to stop traffic.

"What are you doing?" Sadie asked, sounding breathless.

"Just hold on!"

He gunned the engine again.

The sedan behind them did the same.

Just before he reached the section of the road that had washed out, he veered to the left.

He glanced in his rearview mirror.

The other driver hadn't seen the huge gap in the road.

The car headed right toward it.

Trevor threw on brakes and the back of his truck fishtailed, spinning them in a one-eighty.

The next moment, the sedan hit the gigantic hole. The hood dipped, and the vehicle came to a jarring halt, its back wheels spinning useless in the air.

Trevor eased his foot off the brakes and crept toward the scene, remaining cautious. As he got closer, he saw the car had hit the side of the washed-out road hard.

Smoke billowed from beneath the hood.

He threw his truck into Park and climbed out.

Neither of the men inside the car were moving.

Working quickly, he jumped into the hole and jerked the driver's side door opened.

The man remained lifeless inside.

Wasting no time, he grabbed his knife and cut the man's seatbelt off, heaved him over his shoulder, and placed him on the road.

He couldn't reach the other door, so he had to crawl inside the car.

He turned off the engine. But he could still smell gasoline.

The car might go up in flames at any moment.

He had to move quickly.

He cut the other man's seatbelt off also. Then he tried to heave the guy across the seat.

This man was considerably heavier, plus he was dead weight right now.

"Come on," Trevor muttered.

The gasoline smell grew stronger.

The smoke became heavier.

He was on borrowed time.

This car was going to blow.

Sadie held her breath as she looked at the car below. She'd climbed from the truck to see what was happening. To keep an eye on Trevor.

She watched as he disappeared inside.

The scent of gasoline filled the air, and she knew how precarious this was.

Please, Lord . . . protect him.

The man on the ground beside her groaned.

She glanced at him again, but his face didn't trigger any memories.

Then she turned back to Trevor.

Should she jump down there and help him?

Just then, he emerged from the car. He heaved the man over his shoulder.

The sight of it reminded her how strong Trevor was.

Then he lumbered toward the edge of the road and hauled the man onto the blacktop.

He started to hop up onto the street himself.

Before he could, an explosion filled the air.

CHAPTER
THIRTY-NINE

JUST AS TREVOR heard the noise behind him, he propelled himself onto the road.

As he did, he grabbed Sadie.

Threw her back.

Away from any flames.

He landed on top of her, his body shielding hers.

Fire claimed the air—but only for a few seconds.

Then there was the scent of smoke.

He lifted his head and glanced over.

The car was still on fire, but the flames shouldn't reach them now.

He glanced back at Sadie. "Are you okay?"

She stared up at him, appearing dazed. But she nodded. "I'm . . . I'm fine. You?"

He nodded.

"I thought . . . I thought the explosion had gotten you." Worry saturated her voice.

It was touching, really.

"I'm fine," he insisted.

He pulled himself off her, checking her over one more time for injuries.

He saw nothing.

Then he glanced at the two men.

Both still lay motionless.

Sirens came closer. Help was on the way.

He thought for certain that one of these men was the guy who'd shot at him outside the restaurant when Trevor had been following Guy.

Hired hands, probably.

"Do you recognize them?" Trevor asked Sadie.

She brushed her jeans off and came to stand beside him. She peered at their faces but shook her head. "No, unfortunately, I don't."

That was too bad.

Because these men were bad news, and Trevor needed to figure out who had hired them.

At least these two would be out of the picture for a while.

But Trevor felt certain there were more of these operatives out there just waiting to strike.

Most of Sadie's appetite was gone by the time they got to the restaurant.

The police had come as well as paramedics. Both men from the sedan were in critical condition.

She'd seen their faces, and she didn't recognize either of them.

Neither did Trevor.

But those guys had clearly been trying to silence her. Thank goodness for Trevor's quick moves.

Trevor's truck was still a mess, although he'd managed to clean up most of the glass shards. Though it was drivable, he'd said one of his colleagues would secure another vehicle for him—one with a usable windshield.

She grabbed a tortilla chip and dunked it into some freshly made salsa before saying, "Quick thinking back there."

He nodded, though his gaze still appeared troubled. "Thanks. Good to know some of my training paid off."

His words had her curious. "What kind of training did you have?"

His gaze darkened, almost as if he didn't want to answer her question.

Finally, he said, "I was part of an elite group of recruits who went through rigorous training and experiments in order to create what they thought would be the ideal soldier."

"You mean, like Captain America?" Why did she remember who Captain America was? Again, the mind was such a strange thing.

His gaze was humorless. "More like Jason Bourne."

Her eyebrows shot up. "I was only joking."

"I wish it was a joke. Maybe the experiments weren't *exactly* like what was portrayed in those novels and movies, but they were rigorous. Our endurance was tested. They injected us with viruses and other toxins so we could build up immunity. We spent endless days learning languages, how to read people. They worked us hard, so we'd always have the upper hand not only physically but emotionally and intellectually as well."

"I can't even imagine." Her mind race as she tried to picture what it had been like.

On one hand, hard things required sacrifice and effort. On the other hand, should human endurance really be tested like that? Should people in those positions be forced to give up everything—even their own free will?

"It wasn't exactly fun," Trevor continued. "A lot of what happened, I don't remember. There are still side effects I deal with. Tremors mostly and the occasional headache or lapse in memory. My colleagues have reported similar experiences."

"So there are more of you?" Her thoughts continued to race.

"More than a dozen." He nodded. "Most of us, when we left the military, joined the Shadow Agency. It helped us to be around people who understood us."

"No one actually left to start a different life, away from those experiments and missions?"

"A couple people left, wanted to forget everything that happened. Sometimes I wonder how they're doing. The things we went through and experienced were anything but normal."

"Hopefully, they're getting some therapy." Her gaze caught his. "Hopefully, *you've* gotten some therapy."

"I don't know about the ones who got out, but the Shadow Agency has someone on staff we can speak with when needed."

"Most people don't think they need to talk to anyone. Especially men. At least in my experience." Sadie paused and shook her head. "Although I'm not sure exactly how I know that either."

"It's strange what the brain can recall."

"Yes, it is." She dunked another chip into the salsa. "When we were out on dates, did you ever ask me why I came here and started working at the elevator company?"

"I did. You said you'd basically lived a pretty

boring life. That you liked numbers and that you saw a job opening and thought Traverse City would be a fun place to live. You said it was great in the summer, but in the winter this area could be challenging with all the snowfall."

"Did I tell you anything else about myself that might help jog my memory now?"

Before he could answer, their food was delivered, and Trevor asked to say a quick prayer. She agreed, finding a small measure of comfort in the fact he'd wanted to pray. He'd done so before their other meals also.

She instinctively knew that she was a person of faith, and she found reassurance in knowing Trevor was too.

"Can you tell me anything else?" she repeated, not wanting him to forget her question.

He picked up his fork, ready to cut into his beef enchilada. "You were amazing."

Her heart lifted. "What do you mean?"

"You were funny and engaging. You didn't want anything fancy. You were happy going to the beach to watch the sunset or to walk in the sand or to eat fresh cherries you picked up at the local farmer's market."

"That sounds pretty normal, which doesn't match with the other images of myself. The ones where I could be working for a crime boss and trying to bring a decent man down."

His gaze met hers. "A decent man?"

She shrugged. "I mean, it's hard to say for sure. But if I'm trusting my gut, then yes, that's what my gut is telling me."

Trevor shifted in his seat, his gaze turning even more serious. "Listen, Sadie, I wanted to tell you from the start that we'd been dating, but Larchmont told me not to. He clearly knew more of your story than I did."

Sadie shook her head. "I'm sorry it was like that. I really am. I would try to explain myself, but I don't understand anything either."

His gaze remained understanding. "Give yourself some time. I'm still hopeful that your memories will return."

"Before it's too late." Her voice cracked as she said the words.

Because she knew that was what Trevor was thinking.

They needed her to remember certain details about her life sooner rather than later.

They couldn't go on like this forever, and she and Trevor knew that.

At that thought, Sadie picked up her fork and dug into her taco salad.

CHAPTER FORTY

TREVOR PUSHED ASIDE any of the peaceful feelings that tried to fill him.

His conversation with Sadie had been pleasant. It had felt so authentic, as if the two of them were being honest with each other for the first time.

But he knew better than to trust his emotions.

There were still too many unknowns to let down his guard or to believe anything that Sadie said, no matter how much he might want to.

For the rest of their late lunch/early dinner, they talked about Trevor's time in the military, what kind of cherries Sadie liked the best, and why Traverse City had turned out to be an unexpected treasure.

Then Trevor glanced at the time.

They had to go meet that man. If they left now, they would get to the park in time.

Part of him wanted to tell Sadie she shouldn't go. That Trevor should go alone.

But he knew she'd never fall for that. Besides, that guy might not even talk to Trevor.

He dropped some cash on the table instead. "You ready to go?"

Hesitation marred Sadie's gaze, but finally she nodded. "As ready as I'll ever be."

They left, either to find answers or fight for their lives.

Or maybe both.

Sadie's nerves rattled inside her as they headed down the street, the warm wind whipping around them and making her hair fly in the air, certain to become tangled.

What was this man going to say? What if it was something that changed life as she knew it?

Whatever it was, she had to be prepared to hear it. Because learning something about herself was better than not knowing anything at all . . . right?

Sometimes she wasn't so sure of that.

They found a parking space and climbed out, a few stray pebbles of glass falling to the asphalt below.

Trevor would probably keep finding these for a long time.

She brushed aside her rush of nerves as they headed across the street to Clinch Park, a beach on Traverse Bay that had picnic tables, a play area, and lifeguards.

Trevor gently touched the small of her back as they walked.

A shiver raced down Sadie's spine, but she tried to ignore it.

This was no time to develop feelings or even play with the idea of developing feelings. Too much was on the line. Too much was uncertain.

It was a risk she couldn't take.

They reached the beach and found an empty bench with a concrete barrier in front of them.

Plenty of people were strolling around today, many of them tourists who'd come to this area to enjoy its beauty.

On the surface, happiness and peace seemed to permeate the area.

But danger simmered just out of sight.

She and Trevor may have just walked into a situation that could harm them both. That could harm the people around them.

"Maybe we should have told Detective Bennett . . ." she murmured.

"The fewer people who are involved the better," Trevor said.

Sadie could see the merit in his words. They still didn't know who to trust even.

She drew in a shaky breath and continued to glance around. Continued to wait for that man to appear. Continued to imagine what he might tell them.

But as the minutes ticked by, no one came.

"What if this is a trap?" she whispered to Trevor.

He sat beside her, his muscles rigid. He was clearly still on guard.

"Something doesn't feel right, does it?" he murmured.

He could say that again.

Sadie continued to wait, glancing at the time.

This man was ten minutes late.

"How long do we wait?" she asked.

"Let's give it a little longer. Just in case. He could be here right now watching us from a distance and trying to figure out if we brought anyone else with us."

"Good point."

At his words, Sadie glanced around again, searching the people around her for anyone familiar or acting suspiciously.

But she saw no one.

She hoped all this wasn't for nothing.

CHAPTER
FORTY-ONE

MAYBE THIS WAS ALL a scam or maybe they'd been set up.

Trevor was ready to leave.

Then he saw a man walking toward them.

It was him. The man from the elevator. Trevor was nearly certain of it.

Sadie must have felt him stiffen because she suddenly straightened. "He's here, isn't he?"

"Headed our way."

The muscles across his chest tightened as he waited for the man.

Trevor spotted the bulge of the gun tucked inside the man's sweatshirt. In some ways, Trevor couldn't fault the man for coming armed. He had his own gun nestled away, just in case. But he prayed he didn't have to use it. Not here. Not with Sadie and so many civilians around.

The man reached them and sat on the concrete barrier in front of them.

"Didn't think you were going to show up," Trevor started, observing the man coolly.

"I had to make sure it was safe." He remained stiff as he said the words, though to anyone watching this would look like a casual conversation. "Thanks for coming."

"What's this about?" Sadie leaned forward, her voice grim. "Who do you work for?"

The man studied her a moment, an unreadable emotion racing through his gaze. Then he shook his head. "I'll get to that. It'll be better if I explain a few things up front first."

"Go on." Trevor didn't want to draw this out any more than necessary. As he waited, he continued to scan everything around them, looking for trouble. He couldn't afford to let down his guard.

The man looked at Sadie. "My name is Richard Matheson. I've known you for about four years."

Trevor halfway expected this guy to say that he was another secret boyfriend. But he didn't.

"Your name is Sadie," Richard continued. "But your last name isn't Carrington. It is Hayes. Sadie Hayes."

"Where am I from?"

"Indiana."

"Am I an accountant?"

"You *did* study that in school. But you decided that working with numbers wasn't your passion. You wanted something more exciting."

Sadie still sounded cautious as she said, "Tell me more. Do I work for Frederick Moreau?"

"Not really." Richard's expression didn't hint that there was more to the story.

She sucked in a breath as if his words surprised her. "What does that mean?"

"I don't really know how to say this." Richard frowned. "I'm just going to state it outright. Sadie, you work for the FBI, and you were sent here on an undercover assignment to take down any remaining people employed by Frederick Moreau."

Sadie's head spun.

The FBI? What sense did that even make?

It was better than being a criminal, she supposed. But she still had so many questions. So much didn't compute.

"I'm your handler," Richard continued. "I heard what happened to you, and I've been trying to touch base. Then I realized you had amnesia, and you wouldn't remember anything after all."

"Are you the man I used to meet with late at night? My neighbor Victoria told me she saw a man come in the middle of the night."

"Yes. I came to your house when your neighbors were sleeping. It was one of the best times to speak with you and find out if you'd learned anything new. I tried to call you when you were in the hospital, but when you answered, I knew something was wrong. That's why I didn't say anything."

Sadie rubbed her arms, feeling a sudden chill. "From what I've heard, Frederick Moreau is a pretty formidable guy."

"He's in prison, but he still has people out there. You were trying to find out who."

"So I went to work at an elevator company?" She tried to make sense of things.

"We believe someone employed there may also be working for Frederick. You were supposed to figure out who as well as find evidence of what they were doing."

"Okay . . ." She nodded slowly as she tried to comprehend that information. "But it sounds as if one of his guys must have realized what I was doing. Someone tried to kill me in the parking lot."

Richard glanced around again. "I do believe that's what happened. They didn't manage to kill you, but maybe they figured out later that you lost your memory, and that bought them some time."

"Then they realized I might be regaining my memories, and now they're after me again," Sadie finished.

He nodded slowly. "That appears to be the gist of it."

Another question hit her. "What about that man who died? Did I do that?"

"No, we don't believe you did," Richard said. "We believe one of Frederick's guys is responsible."

"That's a relief," Sadie said. "I'd hate to think I'd killed anyone."

"Who was the guy?" Trevor asked.

"We believe he was working for Frederick. Sadie, you discovered that connection and confronted him—that's why you were seen arguing with him."

"Which of Frederick's guys killed him?" Sadie asked.

"We're still trying to figure that out."

"I'm not much good to you if I'm an FBI agent who doesn't have any recollection of my past." Sadie tried not to sound whiny as she said the words, but it was difficult not to. She was in a no-win situation.

"That information is buried somewhere deep inside your brain." Richard's gaze locked with hers. "And we're still hopeful it will emerge."

CHAPTER
FORTY-TWO

SADIE WAS AN FBI AGENT? Trevor's lungs tightened as he tried to discern the truth.

That couldn't be right . . . but what if it was?

After all, so much about her past didn't add up. Maybe that was because it had all either been wiped or fabricated. The FBI had the means of doing that.

And the fact she'd only lived here for six months? That could also match, especially if she was deep undercover. Plus, she had a serious lack of personal items in her apartment. That also fit.

His thoughts continued to race.

"Does this mean anything?" Trevor reached into his pocket and pulled out that set of numbers he had found in Sadie's beach bag.

Richard took the paper from him and scanned it before shaking his head. "Not to me."

"Where did you get that?" Sadie asked, an edge to her voice.

"It was on the ground after your accident, but I didn't think much of it. But now that I know what I know, then maybe this is significant."

She stared at the numbers also but shook her head, her eyes squeezing shut in frustration. "I wish I could remember . . . I mean, what if it's important?"

"Based on the number of digits, the numbers could be bank accounts." Richard continued to study the sheet. "I can check into it."

Sadie looked back up at Trevor again. "Why didn't you mention this earlier?"

"I didn't want to overwhelm you with all the details. What I told you was already a lot."

She opened her mouth as if to argue, but then shut it again and nodded. "Is there anything else that you didn't want to overwhelm me with?"

Trevor's jaw suddenly ached, and he realized he was gritting his teeth. "There was . . . there was blood on your hands when I found you. And I didn't know what that meant so I cleaned your hands and dried them with a towel before paramedics got there."

Her eyes widened. "Is that why I found some blood on my arm?"

He shrugged. "I must not have seen that. You were wearing a coverup—which was surprisingly clean—and I was trying to work quickly before EMTs arrived."

"What did you do with the towel you used to wipe the blood off?" Richard asked.

"My guys have it, just in case we need to test the blood."

"If I didn't kill that man found in the woods and I wasn't bleeding, then why did I have blood on my hands and my arm?" Her face turned paler as she asked the question.

She glanced back and forth from Trevor to Richard, but they both shook their heads and shrugged.

"We'll get to the bottom of it," Trevor reassured her.

Based on the look in her eyes, she didn't believe him.

Trevor couldn't blame her. He was harboring some doubts himself.

"How can we figure out some answers?" Sadie asked.

Richard shook his head, his expression no-nonsense. "You're off the case. There's no way we can let you continue, not with your head injury and your memory issues. Just wouldn't be wise on many different levels."

"I have to agree with him," Trevor said.

Traitor. But Sadie kept that thought to herself.

"I'm going to be a target until we figure this out." She knew they couldn't deny her words. Someone was already after her, and they weren't going to stop until she was silenced—for good.

"We'll assign agents to protect you," Richard said. "But for now, we need to get you out of this area to somewhere safe until this ordeal blows over."

Leaving was the last thing Sadie wanted to do. She knew she'd be a liability here. She didn't deny that fact. But still . . . this was her life. This had been her case. Even if she couldn't remember the details, she wanted to be here.

She glanced at Trevor, curious as to his reaction.

His shoulders swelled at Richard's words. "I am protecting her."

"You seem to be doing a fine job, all things considered." He paused. "Although, I've looked into you. Former military. But there's not much about you post military. Only that you work for that security group."

"Not much else to know. I try to keep my nose clean."

Richard continued to eye him. "I can't help but wonder if there's more to you than that."

Trevor shrugged. "I don't know what you want me to say."

Richard stared at Trevor another moment before looking back at Sadie, seeming to let the conversation drop. "The best way to figure this out is to get our asset out of here and go to a Plan B."

"There has to be another way . . ." Sadie muttered.

Something crossed Richard's gaze, but he kept his mouth shut. He had a thought. An idea. Sadie was certain of it.

"What are you thinking?" she asked.

He pressed his lips together and shook his head as if unwilling to say it.

"Richard . . . please." She stared at the man. "I'm not fragile. Just because I lost my memory doesn't mean I'm an idiot."

"That's not what I'm trying to get at. It's just that . . ."

"Then let me help."

He let out a long breath. "Tonight there's a company party. At Frank's place."

"What about it?"

"The last time we spoke, you thought something was going to go down at the event. Maybe if we can get an agent in there . . ."

"How are you going to get a stranger into an

office party? It doesn't even make sense." Sadie had to somehow get through to him.

"Maybe they can be disguised as a server."

"Kind of cliché, don't you think?" She let her head fall to the side as she stared at him. "Let me go."

"That's a bad idea," Richard muttered. "A very bad idea."

She somehow needed to convince him that that was a great idea. But she knew this would be an uphill battle.

CHAPTER
FORTY-THREE

TREVOR WASN'T sure what to think about Sadie's idea.

On one hand, it had merit. She made the most sense. She would have been invited to the party anyway.

But on the other hand, she may have been close to figuring out who was working with Frederick, and that would put her in a direct line of fire.

"What if you have agents stationed outside?" she asked. "And I can call you at the first hint of danger?"

"There's no guarantee we would get there in time even if we were stationed outside."

"I think I can do this," Sadie said. "I can bring Trevor with me, and he'll watch my back."

Part of Trevor was surprised she would even

want him there, knowing everything she did. But maybe she'd made that statement simply out of desperation.

"I just don't think this is going to work," Richard said.

"I promise, I won't mess it up. If something's going down, I need to be there to figure out what it is. Trevor will protect me."

"I just don't understand how you'll figure out what's going on if you can't remember anything." Richard's expression turned even stonier.

"You can brief me on everything that I've told you. Then I'll know."

Richard's jaw tightened, and he frowned. But it appeared he was considering it.

Finally, he turned back to Sadie and nodded. "Fine. I'll brief you. I'll have to set you up with a wire so we can hear everything that's going on." Then he looked at Trevor. "But we can't let this go south. It's already a risky operation, and Sadie's amnesia only makes this more complicated."

From the sound of it, Richard didn't know that Trevor was the one who'd ultimately brought down Frederick. It made sense. That information was highly classified, so classified that not even the feds should know.

Trevor offered a curt nod. "I understand. You can count on me."

If Frederick's minions were still up to no good, he wanted to know what they were doing.

Maybe tonight he would know once and for all.

―――――

An hour later, Sadie had been briefed.

The FBI believed that someone at Sleeping Bear Elevator was secretly working for Frederick and using the company to smuggle drugs into the country. Intel had led them to the elevator company, but they still needed proof.

That was where Sadie had come in.

She'd been instructed to infiltrate the company and snoop around for answers. Hired as an accountant, she had access to the company's financials.

The first few months had been slow, and she had been using her relationship with Guy to try to find out more information.

Their initial suspect was Frank, but she'd found no evidence that he was behind it.

The VP, Mark Stuart, and COO, Juan Blevins, were also suspects.

Armed with this new information, she'd gone to the store and picked out a black dress for tonight. Trevor had gotten a nice pair of black slacks with a blue shirt. Then they'd spent thirty minutes getting ready so they could look presentable.

Sadie's eyes widened when she stepped out of the bathroom and saw Trevor standing there.

He certainly did look handsome with every hair in place, his face freshly shaven, and his clothes clean and pressed.

If only she could rewrite the history between them . . .

Every time she looked at him, her heart began to thump out of control.

Based on the way he stared back at her, he felt the same thing.

The two of them had found each other only for this uncrossable chasm to form.

It seemed like such a wasted opportunity.

But Sadie had a hard time seeing how the two of them could ever trust each other again. Not after all the deception each of them had been through.

"You look beautiful." Trevor had a wispiness to his voice that sounded sincere.

"You don't look bad yourself." She paused in front of him, resisting the urge to straighten his collar. Touching him right now was a terrible idea.

He lowered his gaze. "You sure you're up for this?"

Sadie nodded, probably a little too quickly. "Of course. I need to do this. It's the only way I'll get on with my life . . . whatever that's going to look like."

She had more answers now, but the thought of

continuing as Special Agent Sadie Hayes left her feeling empty and confused, like that wasn't her place anymore. Maybe that would change. But maybe it wouldn't.

Kai met them in the room, and Sadie took a step back, realizing she was standing entirely too close to Trevor.

Kai would go along with them tonight and work with the FBI to monitor the situation.

"Did I interrupt something?" Kai glanced back and forth between them.

"No." Sadie and Trevor both answered at the same time. "Of course not."

"Okay then." Kai cleared his throat. "If you guys are ready, let's get you wired, and then we can go."

CHAPTER
FORTY-FOUR

TREVOR STILL HAD some reservations about this. But he prayed that everything would go well. That Sadie would remain safe. That they could find answers and bring down Frederick once and for all.

They pulled to a stop in front of a large house with a U-shaped driveway in front of it. The place was white, with two stories and a wide front porch. Neat flowerbeds, a freshly cut lawn, and amazing views of Grand Traverse Bay rounded out the look.

The party was fancy, but not fancy enough for a valet. Instead, as they pulled up, the front door opened, and Frank stepped out.

"I was hoping you'd make it, Sadie," he called.

Trevor slipped his keys into his pocket as he climbed from the car Kai had let him borrow. Then he and Sadie ascended six steps to the sweeping front porch.

"Thanks for letting me come, even after everything that's happened." Sadie smiled at her boss.

"Of course." Frank touched her shoulder. "We're just glad to have you with us."

The man sounded sincere, Trevor realized. But was he?

Trevor wasn't sure who at this party could be trusted. As far as he was concerned, everyone was a suspect.

His only comfort was knowing six agents were stationed outside, in addition to Kai.

Not only had Sadie been wired, but so had he.

They stepped through the foyer and into a large living room where employees from Sleeping Bear Elevator mingled. A long table had been set up across the back of the room with hors d'oeuvres that people enjoyed as they socialized.

As Sadie walked into the room several people turned, surprise flashing in their gazes.

He and Sadie had a plan in place for tonight.

He hoped everything worked out accordingly, because now that they were here, it was showtime.

Trevor needed to watch everyone closely and see if he could figure out who might be guilty.

Reading people was something he'd been trained to do.

"Everyone," Frank announced, tapping his spoon against a glass. "We're so happy to have Sadie here with us tonight."

The guests broke out in applause.

"Thank you." She waved a hand, self-conscious at the attention. "It's good to be here."

April stepped from the crowd and gently touched her arm. "Are you feeling better?"

"I am." Sadie smiled softly. "In fact, my memories have returned."

Gasps of surprise went around the room.

Unfortunately, the memories hadn't returned. But he and Sadie wanted the bad guy to think they had.

Because it might force his or her hand. Make them shake in their boots just a little bit.

However, the move was risky, and Trevor hoped that it paid off.

Sadie spent the next hour mingling and eating and trying to appear halfway normal.

She had been given a dossier of all the employees who worked for Sleeping Bear Elevator, and she'd memorized each of their names and what they did at the company.

It had been necessary to know those details if she wanted to sell the fact that her memories had returned. People might be able to excuse a few blips here and there, but she needed to sell this if she wanted answers.

Whoever was behind the incidents happening to her needed to be smoked out.

As she talked, Trevor stayed close. He was surprisingly attentive and a good actor.

The one person she hadn't seen yet was Guy. She was surprised he wasn't here, but she had to wonder after their confrontation earlier today if he was moping or staying away for that purpose. She couldn't really be sure.

As she talked to various people, she couldn't help but wonder if one of them was a killer. Part of her didn't want to believe anyone here could be dangerous. But someone here made the most sense.

She needed to figure out who.

Frank Bolster. Former pro golfer turned elevator company owner. He had access to everything but no record of criminal activity.

April Smith. Office manager. Dating a man who'd been arrested three times on drug charges.

Mark Stuart. Vice President. Owned two homes and was in a considerable amount of debt trying to pay for them.

Juan Blevins. COO. World traveler with many connections. Seen near the supply room before the fire. Was one of his connections Frederick?

Stephanie Lansky. Receptionist. Single with three cats. She didn't seem the type.

Agents were stationed around the perimeter of the house, except on the side where the lake was. A sheer cliff stretched there, and it would be impossible for anyone to get in the actual yard without being noticed.

The situation wasn't ideal.

But she was praying for the best.

On a break in her conversation with April, Sadie glanced over.

Frank was looking at something on his phone and frowning. Then he glanced around as if searching for someone or something.

"Strange," Trevor whispered in her ear.

Her thoughts exactly. Why did he look so antsy?

She knew Trevor would also keep an eye on him, see if he did anything else that seemed suspicious.

Just as April started talking to her about a big conference they had coming up in Vegas next month, the door opened.

Guy stepped in.

Her heart lurched into her throat.

So he *had* come.

Trevor moved in closer as if he sensed her rising tension.

Right away, Guy's gaze found them. Then he

blurted, "I know the two of you are up to something, and I'm here to figure out what!"

CHAPTER
FORTY-FIVE

TREVOR BRACED himself for whatever Guy would say or do next.

Everyone stared at them as Guy's words seemed to hang in the room.

I know the two of you are up to something, and I'm here to figure out what.

Trevor stepped closer to him. One look at the man's glazed eyes, and hearing his slurred words and sloppy motions, Trevor knew he had been drinking.

"I think you need to sober up," Trevor said.

"Don't tell me to sober up." Guy's head wobbled almost as if he might pass out.

Frank appeared beside them also. "Guy, I'm not sure it's a good idea for you to be here. I'm going to call for a ride home for you."

Guy pulled his keys from his pockets. "I don't want to leave. When I do want to leave, I can drive myself."

Trevor snatched the keys from him. "You're not getting on the road again in your current state."

Guy's eyes narrowed. "You're not the boss of me. You can't tell me what to do."

Guy tried to grab the keys back, but Trevor placed them in his pocket.

That only made Guy more upset. "I followed you today. Did you know that?"

Trevor's breath caught. "Are you stalking Sadie?"

Trevor needed to turn this back around on Guy and deflect this conversation.

"Something's not adding up!" Guy said as he swayed. "I'm going to figure out what if it's the last thing I do."

"Why were your shoes muddy on the day of the fire?" Trevor asked. "Are you the one who set it?"

"What? Why would I do that?" Guy's lips parted in surprise.

"You tell me."

"I was doing some investigating. Hunting around for answers. But not setting fires!" His eyes narrowed. "Maybe *you* set the fire!"

Frank took Guy's arm, ready to lead him away from the crowd where he was making a scene.

Everyone in the room watched the interaction. How could they not?

"You don't need to be here acting like this, Guy," Frank said. "Let's get you somewhere you can sober up."

"I haven't even been drinking!"

"I think we all know that's not true," Frank said.

"I haven't!" Spittle flew from Guy's mouth as he said the words.

The next instant, his eyes glazed. His body wavered.

Trevor braced himself, realizing that something wasn't right.

Then Guy fell to the floor, his body completely still.

———

Sadie watched in horror as Guy hit the floor and was out cold.

"Somebody call 911!" Frank yelled.

Several people grabbed their phones. Sadie also grabbed hers and texted Kai, letting him know what was going on. They'd need to know when the ambulance arrived.

Kai promised to let Richard know also. They'd been listening, but it had been hard to make out everything that was happening, he'd said.

Had Guy really passed out because he was drunk? Or was there more to it?

Sadie didn't smell any alcohol on his breath.

What had Guy meant? Had he really not been drinking? What else would cause him to act like this?

Trevor knelt on one side of him and Frank on the other. They checked his pulse, his breathing.

Then another thought hit her.

What if he'd been poisoned? Or drugged?

Because if Guy had been following them today, then he might have seen something he wasn't supposed to see.

If Frederick's men were watching everything, then they might want to silence Guy also.

If that was the case, she supposed they could rule Guy out as a suspect.

But this wasn't what she wanted.

Not even close.

She stood to the side, knowing it was a bad idea for too many people to surround him right now. Instead, she lifted up a prayer.

Trevor glanced over and met Sadie's gaze. Even though they didn't say a word, a conversation took place between them.

He knew something was up also.

Then his gaze wandered above her.

He whispered something to Frank and then rose.

He approached Sadie.

"I saw someone upstairs," he whispered. "I'm going to go check it out."

A chill washed over her before she muttered, "Be careful."

"I will. You be careful too. I don't want anything happening to you."

Sadie could hear the sincerity in his voice. It was then she realized that even with the history between them—the good and the bad—she truly did care about him.

She could easily believe his boss had put him up to most of this.

Did that mean the two of them could have a chance together? She couldn't say that. There was so much she couldn't even remember.

But her feelings for the man were clear. They were there, and they were strong. Real.

She watched as he disappeared. Everyone still faced Guy, but now they were murmuring among themselves.

Juan Blevins edged closer. "I always thought he was a little unhinged. It wasn't my idea to hire him."

"Unhinged?"

Juan nodded. "I saw the way he looked at you, and I knew he was going to be trouble. But without ample reason to fire him . . . we were kind of stuck."

"Has he always acted so brazen?" Sadie asked.

"He likes to live large. I knew his cockiness would

get the best of him. I just didn't know he was drinking so heavily. That he'd take things this far. He is always trying to master the art of closing the deal—in business and relationships."

"Excuse me a moment." Sadie's head pounded, and she needed to be by herself if she was going to make sense of everything. She was trying to think clearly right now and failing. "Where is the bathroom?"

He pointed to a hallway in the distance.

She thanked him and then headed that way, anxious for a moment by herself.

She reached the bathroom door and twisted the knob.

It was unlocked.

But before she stepped inside, a footstep sounded behind her.

CHAPTER
FORTY-SIX

TREVOR WALKED along the upstairs hallway, looking for the stranger who had been watching everything from above.

He wasn't an employee at Sleeping Bear Elevator. So who was he? And what was he doing here?

That was what Trevor needed to figure out.

Gun in hand, he walked down the dark hallway. He didn't want to call any attention to himself, so he hoped nobody had seen him slip this way. They all seem to be focused on Guy anyway.

He could already hear sirens in the distance, coming this way.

He wasn't sure what had happened to the man. But he suspected he had been either drugged or poisoned. The good news was that he still had a pulse, and his breathing was still steady. And if the paramedics got here in time, Trevor thought Guy would be okay.

He peered into the first room he passed, but darkness stared back. He flipped on the light switch, cleared the room, and then moved on.

He did the same at each doorway he came to.

He stepped inside the last room. It appeared to be the master bedroom. He searched the perimeter. The closet. The master bath. Under the bed.

Nothing.

Where had that man gone?

He glanced up at the patio doors on the other side of the room.

The balcony. It was the only place he hadn't checked.

Cautiously, he walked toward it, and slowly opened the door.

As he did, someone lunged at him.

Trevor hit the floor, and the gun skittered from his hand.

It was a man—someone he didn't recognize.

But the guy was on top of him, and his hands circled Trevor's throat.

If Trevor didn't act quickly, then he wasn't going to walk away from this.

Before Sadie could turn, a hand slipped around her mouth, clamping her lips shut.

Then she heard a click and felt something hard press into her ribs.

A gun.

"Make a sound, and I'll kill you. Do you understand?"

She forced herself to nod.

Did she recognize that voice? She wasn't sure yet.

"We're going to walk to the end of this hallway without making a scene," the man continued.

A tremble captured her muscles, but she moved forward.

If she started fighting back, would she remember all the defense moves she'd no doubt learned as an FBI agent?

She wasn't sure. Considering the fact the man had a gun, she didn't want to risk it.

She shouldn't have gone to the bathroom.

With Trevor upstairs confronting that other man and everyone else distracted with Guy, she had thought it would be okay.

She'd been wrong.

The gun pressed harder into her side as they walked to the back of the house.

"Open the door," the man ordered.

With trembling hands, she did as he asked.

Then they stepped onto the patio.

She halfway expected to see someone else out here, but there was no one.

Just the two of them.

Overhead, she heard a thump and froze.

Was that Trevor? Was he in trouble also? Exactly how many enemies did they have here?

"What are you going to do with me out here?" she asked.

"You'll see." He continued to push her forward, closer to the cliff that awaited in the distance.

Her thoughts raced.

A gunshot wound would be too obvious.

Falling off that cliff?

Someone might think it was an accident or maybe even suicide.

At once, what this man was planning became all too clear.

"You're not going to get away with this," she said.

He let out a chuckle. "I think I am."

"All so you can secretly transport drugs? Why the elevator company, of all places?"

"It made the most sense. The shipments are large, with plenty of places to conceal the things that we need to move. It was a win-win."

This guy obviously thought it all through.

They got closer and closer to the cliff.

Sadie wanted to turn. Wanted to see this man's face. Wanted to ask more questions.

Then the man stopped. Shoved something in her hand.

"Take this," he ordered.

She looked down and saw the pill in her hand.

No way was she going to swallow that.

She flung her hand, and the pill toppled over the cliff.

"You shouldn't have done that," the man growled. "We're going to have to do this my way this time."

Then he grabbed something from his pocket. The next moment, he shoved it in her mouth.

A pill.

He was trying to force her to swallow it.

His hand clamped over her mouth. Sadie could feel the pill on her tongue, beginning to dissolve.

As panic rose in her, she reminded herself not to do anything rash.

She reminded herself that, whatever she did, she could *not* swallow.

CHAPTER
FORTY-SEVEN

TREVOR SHIFTED his body weight and raised his knees.

He kicked the man off him.

The attacker fell to the floor, and Trevor was instantly on top of him, pinning his arms to his side.

As he looked at the man's face, he confirmed he'd never seen the guy before. So who was he?

He expected the man to fight back, but his efforts were futile. Trevor easily had him pinned.

"Who are you?" Trevor demanded.

"Who are *you*?"

"I'm someone who's protecting Sadie. But I think you already know that."

"I think we both know there's more to your story."

Trevor didn't react to his statement. "Are you the one who's been trying to kill her?"

The man's eyes widened. "Kill her? No. I'm not trying to kill her. I don't know what you're talking about."

"Then you need to start talking before the FBI comes running. They're stationed all around this house."

"The feds? There's no need to bring the feds into this. I'm Larry, Frank's cousin."

"Are you the one behind whatever's going on at the company?"

"Frank asked me to keep an eye on things so that's what I've been doing. I'm trying to figure out if someone is using his company as a front for something illegal."

Trevor didn't hear any deceit in his voice.

He loosened his grip just slightly on the man and leaned back. "Keep talking."

"Frank suspects that someone at his company is using the shipments to transport drugs. Possibly fentanyl. I used to be a corrections officer at the jail, so I have a little background in law enforcement. He asked me to see if I can figure out who's behind this."

"Did you think it was Sadie?"

"I questioned if it could be her for a while," Larry said. "Because she was definitely acting like she was up to something. Snooping around and asking strange questions. Plus, there is a matter of her not truly having a past. That always sends up red flags."

"Sadie isn't behind this," Trevor said.

"I know that now. So I'm trying to figure out who else it might be. I was supposed to simply linger in the background tonight and see what I could find out. But when I heard the commotion downstairs, I peeked my head out. That's when you saw me."

Trevor thought his story made sense.

"Are you the one who shot at me?"

"Shot at you?" Larry made a face. "No, I only watched everything from a distance. I swear."

Trevor rose to his feet, his hands on his hips. "Is there anything else you can tell me? Because whoever is behind this has set their sights on Sadie. I need to keep her alive."

As soon as he said the words, he heard a noise below.

When he glanced down at the bay, he saw two people standing dangerously close to the cliff.

One of them was Sadie.

Sadie shook her head back and forth, determined to get the man's hand from her mouth.

She still felt the pill on her tongue. The tablet was dissolving.

Her head was spinning. Her heart racing even faster than before. Her lungs constricted as if unable to take on any air.

"Just stop fighting it," the man said. "It will be easier that way."

Something about his words ignited something in her.

In two seconds flat, she opened her mouth and her teeth dug into the man's skin.

He yelped and jerked his hand away.

As soon as he did, she spit the remainder of the pill onto the grass.

She started to run.

Before she could, he grabbed her arm and jerked her toward him.

She hit the ground, her forehead colliding with a rock at the edge of the lawn.

At once, flashes of memory began to appear in her mind again.

Memories of struggling. Arguing.

With this man.

In the woods.

Then another man had appeared.

The man who died.

But she hadn't killed him. In fact, she'd tried to help him.

The man in front of her had killed him. Stabbed him.

Her gun had been out of bullets, so she'd had to run.

She'd managed to get away. To throw a shirt on over her bloody hands. To jump in her car. Thankfully, nothing had gotten on her swimsuit or coverup.

She'd gone to the beach to meet Trevor until she and Richard could speak that evening.

As her thoughts cleared, Sadie glanced up.

Her breath caught when she recognized the face staring back at her.

Bart Tatum.

The delivery driver.

The one who was only in the office a couple of times a week.

The jovial brother she'd never had. That was how they'd always joked.

Everyone in the office thought of him as a brother.

He was the one behind this the whole time?

"I know what you're thinking," he muttered. "You're surprised I could do something like this."

"You were in the perfect position, weren't you? You had access to all the shipments. But you stayed below the radar the whole time."

He nodded, a smug expression on his face. "That's right, but you were about to blow it all. I hit you with the car, hoping that would do you in. Then you got amnesia. It was perfect timing. Until I realized your memories might return. That's when I knew I had to protect this operation at all costs. The little fire stunt I pulled didn't work, so I had to resort to other measures."

He raised his gun at her.

"You don't have to do this," she murmured.

"I'm not going to do this. Because you're going to jump."

She looked over the cliff, and the breath left her lungs when she saw just how far below the rocky shore was.

"No," she muttered.

He cocked the weapon. "Yes."

"You're not going to shoot me. If you do it will be obvious that you're involved. Everyone will know."

He snarled. "If I can't shoot *you*, then I'll shoot *your friend*. You can fight this all you want, but I'm going to get what I want, one way or another."

She heard the conviction in his voice.

He meant the words.

Even though she knew Trevor could protect himself, the thought of something happening to him made a heaviness press into her chest.

That was the last thing that she wanted.

"Jump," Bart said.

She glanced down again, and her head began to swirl.

The drug . . . it was beginning to take effect. Beginning to play with her logic and reasoning.

If Sadie didn't get a grip quickly, she didn't know what was going to happen.

CHAPTER
FORTY-EIGHT

TREVOR KNEW he had little time to help Sadie.

He peered over the balcony and saw the patio below.

Without wasting any more time, he hurtled himself over the balcony railing and landed on his feet.

He paused only a couple of seconds to find his balance, and then he took off toward the figures in the distance.

At once, he saw the gun in the man's hand.

Saw it raised toward Sadie.

Trevor didn't have much time to act.

"Stop!" he yelled.

The man turned toward him, swinging his gun his way.

Trevor had seen this man before.

He was . . . the delivery driver at Sleeping Bear Elevator. What was his name again? Bart, if he remembered correctly.

"You should have stayed out of this," the man said.

"You need to let her go," Trevor said. "Killing her isn't going to solve anything."

Where was his backup? The feds and Kai should have come by now. What could possibly be stopping them?

"You're right," Bart said. "I don't need to just do away with Sadie. For that reason, I'm glad you could join us. Why don't you go stand beside her at the cliff?"

This guy couldn't be serious. Yet he was.

Trevor raised his hands and slowly walked toward him.

"You're not going to get away with this," Trevor said.

"You let me worry about that. You two are going to jump together."

Trevor glanced down and felt a cool breeze sweep over the water and touch his face.

It was a long way down. Probably twenty-five feet. It wasn't soft sand either. It was jagged and rocky.

Come on, backup! Where are you?

So far, nothing was going according to plan.

"Why are you doing all this?" Trevor asked instead. "You think Frederick would do this for you? I can answer that question. He wouldn't. You're just his scapegoat. He's using you."

Trevor watched Bart's eyes narrow.

He'd hit a nerve by saying those words.

"I would do anything for Frederick, and he would do anything for me."

"If he ever gets out of prison, you're the first one he'll do away with. He doesn't like to share the spotlight."

"Why do you talk about it as if you know him?"

"Because I do," Trevor said. "I'm the one who put him away."

"Freeze! FBI!"

Finally, backup had arrived.

Trevor glanced at Bart. Saw him contemplating what to do.

Then he felt Sadie sway beside him.

The next moment, her body went limp, and she slipped toward the cliff.

Sadie felt herself falling, and her eyes jerked open.

The drug . . . she realized. It was messing with her.

Even though she'd tried not to absorb much, it was too late.

Now it might kill her anyway.

"No!" she heard someone yell above her.

Her body stiffened.

Nothing but air was beneath her.

Do something, Sadie! Pull yourself together!

Her eyes jerked open.

Sadie realized she'd slipped off the cliff.

She wouldn't survive the fall. She was certain of it.

Her arms flailed.

Then her fingers caught something.

A ledge, she realized.

Her body jerked to a stop, her arms aching in their sockets in the process.

She blew out a breath.

But at least she was still alive.

She would take that to the alternative.

She glanced down.

She still had a lot farther to fall.

Which was why she couldn't let go, no matter how slippery the rock was.

"Sadie!"

She looked up and saw Trevor leaning down.

"You're okay?"

"For now." Her voice quivered as she said the words.

Her head began to spin again.

"He forced a pill on me," she told Trevor. "Maybe fentanyl. My brain and heart and lungs are going crazy right now. I feel like I'm not even in control of myself."

She looked up and saw the fear glimmering in Trevor's eyes.

That was when she knew she really was in trouble.

CHAPTER
FORTY-NINE

TREVOR QUICKLY GLANCED AT BART.

The FBI had taken him into custody.

Now Richard and Kai stood on either side of Trevor, trying to figure out how to rescue Sadie before it was too late.

If they could get equipment to her, that would be one thing.

But there was no time for that.

"Hold onto my legs!" he told Richard and Kai. "Lower me until I can grab her."

"We can bring some rappelling equipment—" Richard started.

"There's no time," Trevor said. "By the time it gets here, it will be too late."

No one argued with him. They knew he spoke the truth.

"We need to move," Trevor said. "Now!"

Trevor dropped to his knees and stretched forward.

Richard and Kai grabbed his legs. Then he inched toward the cliff.

Sadie was far enough down that Trevor couldn't reach her with just his arms. He needed another two feet.

As he began to move down lower, his equilibrium shifted.

It was too far of a drop. If they slipped . . .

Trevor prayed this worked. Otherwise, he and Sadie would both be goners.

If Kai and Richard somehow let him slip out of their grasp, he would tumble to the shore below and take Sadie with him.

He couldn't let that happen.

They hadn't come this far to fail now.

Sadie let out a cry below him as one of her hands slipped.

"Hold onto the rock!" he yelled. "Reach for it. You can do it."

Her eyes were wide as she stared up at him. Then she reached forward and managed to grab hold of the ledge again.

Good.

If only everything wasn't so moist and slippery

here. It made the whole situation even more precarious.

"I'm going to reach for you," he told her. "I'm going to grab your wrists. Then we're going to pull you up. It's not going to be comfortable, but it's the only way we can get through this. Do you understand?"

"I understand. Yes. Please, just help me."

"I need to go a little farther down," he yelled to the guys above him.

The cliff edge was already at his waist. Once he went beyond his waist, it became even more precarious as his body didn't bend the right way.

He felt Richard and Kai's hands gripping his ankles. Felt the strain on his muscles and body.

Finally, they lowered him enough so he could reach her.

"On the count of three, I'm going to slip my hands beneath yours. There's going to be a brief second where you're going to feel like you're not holding onto anything. But I've got you. Okay?"

"O . . . okay." But her voice trembled with fear.

Trevor swallowed hard, sucking in a deep breath. He lifted a quick prayer before he grabbed her wrists.

She gasped as he touched her. Then she fell an inch before his hold on her took traction.

She jerked to a stop and dangled below him.

"I've got you," he told her.

Relief washed over her features.

But almost as soon as he said the words, he felt both of them begin to slip down and either Richard or Kai yelled above him.

That was when Trevor realized that something was wrong.

Sadie felt herself falling again.

At once, a memory hit her.

A memory of chasing down a killer in the Appalachian Mountains.

The man had pushed her off a cliff, but she had caught herself.

She'd managed to hang on for an hour.

That was how long it had taken her partner to find her and get her help.

But she'd survived that.

She could survive this too.

They lurched to a stop.

Despite the downward momentum, Trevor's grip on her never loosened.

As she stared up at him now, her pulse raced even more quickly.

This man was willing to do whatever it took to protect her. That was rare in today's world.

Then more memories filled her. Memories of

meeting Trevor on the shore. Memories of how she felt when he flashed that smile at her. As they shared a basket of cherries on the seashore while watching the sunset. As they sat and talked about nothing yet talked about everything at the same time.

Those moments . . . they had felt real.

Probably because they *were* real.

Despite all the subterfuge, what had developed between them was anything but fake.

Despite what they had been through, Sadie knew that her feelings for this man were strong.

"You okay?" Trevor asked.

Sadie nodded, realizing just how many of her memories were beginning to return.

"Pull us up," Trevor said.

"Sorry, the ground started to give beneath us!" Kai called down. "We've got you now."

Slowly, they began to ascend the cliff, inch by inch, centimeter by centimeter.

At least they weren't falling anymore.

People talked above them. Occasionally, faces peered down. The lights of a police car or ambulance flashed in the distance.

Another shiver raced through her.

"Just keep looking at me," Trevor told her.

That was what Sadie did. Their gazes locked, and reassurance beamed from his gaze.

At the moment, she felt as if that was all she needed.

Trevor had done everything within his power to protect her, and he hadn't let her down yet.

She knew with certainty he wouldn't let her down now either.

Trevor drew back as Kai and Richard slid him across the lawn.

Once Trevor was on solid ground, the two men took Sadie's arms and pulled her the rest of the way to safety.

Sadie collapsed there as she tried to gain control of her breathing.

That had been close. Too close.

As much as she wanted to rejoice or to embrace Trevor or to tell him about all the realizations that she'd had, she couldn't do that.

Her heart was pounding so fast she felt as if she might go into cardiac arrest. She couldn't breathe. Her skin crawled.

The drug, she realized.

She'd just conquered one danger, but an even bigger one loomed and threatened to take her life now.

CHAPTER FIFTY

"HE FORCED her to take some drug, probably fentanyl!" Trevor shouted as he knelt beside Sadie. "She needs help."

Paramedics surrounded them, moving him out of the way. Helplessness filled him as they bent over Sadie, spraying something into her nose.

Narcan.

Trevor held his breath as he waited. Would it work?

The next instant, she gulped in a deep breath and sat straight up, almost as if life had suddenly returned to her.

Relief swept through him.

Trevor wanted to rush to her side, but he gave the paramedics room to work. Sadie's health and well-being was more important right now.

He didn't care about the cuts and scrapes on his own chest from being dragged along the cliff face. Didn't care about the ache in his wrist or his throbbing jaw from the fight inside.

Only Sadie.

"Sorry it took us so long to get here." Richard appeared beside him. "Someone called the cops on us, and we were temporarily detained."

He glanced at the agent. "You didn't tell the local police what the FBI was doing?"

Richard's gaze darkened. "In this case, no, we didn't. I didn't think it would make a difference. I believe that Bart was the one behind that. He knew what was going to happen, and he tried to do everything to stop it, in the process hoping to impress Frederick."

"That sounds about right," Trevor said. "What he doesn't realize is that the only person Frederick thinks about is himself."

"Doesn't matter now. He's going to be sent away for a long time."

"Good." Trevor looked over at the man and saw him sitting handcuffed on a bench, FBI agents on either side.

On the patio, various Sleeping Bear Elevator employees stood around, watching in shock as everything unfolded.

Maybe they could put this behind them and move forward now.

Sadie should be off this case.

So should Trevor, for that matter.

What did that mean for their future? He had no idea.

But he hoped he and Sadie could talk about it as soon as she felt better.

Sadie heard someone knock at the door to her hospital room, and she called, "Come in!"

A smile spread across her face when Trevor stepped inside.

She'd hoped it would be him.

"Hey, there." He slowly strode closer, his movements a little stiffer than usual.

Probably from the struggle they'd both been through, as well as his valiant rescue of her on the cliff.

"Hey." She watched as he paused beside her bed. "It seems ironic that we're back here at the hospital again. This is where it all started . . . the second time, at least."

His fingers gently brushed her arm. "That's right. The second time. But I'm hoping we might be able to start all over again for a third time."

Her grin widened. "I like that idea."

The two of them exchanged a lingering look that promised more.

They had a lot they needed to talk about later. But it appeared both of them wanted another chance to see where a relationship between them would lead. Considering their careers and schedules, Sadie knew it might be difficult.

But she also knew that with some effort, a relationship between them could work if that was what they both truly wanted.

She looked away and cleared her throat before she got ahead of herself. Four dates, she reminded herself. That was all the two of them had. Everything that had happened between them made it feel more like four months.

She shifted her thoughts as more pressing questions came to mind. "Any updates you've heard about?"

Trevor shrugged. "Probably what you mostly already know since Richard has already talked to you."

"I heard Guy is going to be okay." Richard had told her the man's water had been drugged. He'd been a distraction from everything else going on.

"Yes, that's good news. I mean, the man was annoying, but . . ."

"I'm glad he'll be okay." Sadie nodded.

"Bart was behind this the whole time. He wasn't a part of Moreau's crime ring when I infiltrated it. But he moved in and quickly became Frederick's right-hand man. He really was a delivery driver, and Frederick encouraged him to look for ways to bring drugs into the country. Bart discovered when Sleeping Bear Elevator got their shipments in from Switzerland, that the elevator equipment would be perfect for smuggling drugs laced with fentanyl."

"A pretty clever plan, I suppose." Sadie shrugged. "Not one worth killing over, however."

"I agree. Apparently, those numbers I found from your beach bag were invoices."

"Yes, that's right." Sadie had remembered some of those details. "I figured out what shipments had drugs, and I was about to hand that intel over to Richard when I met him later."

"Then Bart caught on to what you were doing and tried to silence you." His gaze darkened.

"I remembered a house fire when I was a child." Sadie's voice caught. "My parents were killed, but I survived. I mentioned it one day in the office—not the details. I didn't want to blow my cover. But using parts of the truth in a cover story is usually the best way to go."

"I agree.

"Bart must have overheard it. Maybe he thought

the fire would trigger a memory or maybe he just wanted to scare me. I'm not sure."

"I imagine that was traumatic."

Her throat squeezed at the memories. "Afterward, I went to live with an aunt."

He clasped her hand. "I'm sorry to hear all that."

She heaved in a deep breath, trying not to feel overwhelmed as pieces of her life filled her mind. "Mostly, I've been remembering the details of my case. I remember linking Bart to all these crimes. I found him meeting with John Breckenridge in the woods. They were arguing."

"John wasn't here to kayak . . ." Trevor raised his eyebrows warily.

"No, he wasn't. He was here to pick up a shipment, but Bart decided he couldn't trust him. He stabbed him, and I rushed over, trying to help. It was too late. It was that same day I was hit by the car. I had planned on meeting Richard that night to tell him. I didn't get the chance." Her gut twisted at the memories.

"Did they ever tell you who altered the medical orders and almost killed you here in the hospital?" Trevor asked.

"It turns out Bart's girlfriend is a nurse here. She was never my nurse. But Bart talked her into going into the system and changing those orders. The entire process is pretty complicated, but Bart had one of his guys take down the firewall just long enough for her to make the change. She's also been arrested and is facing charges."

Trevor stared down at her. "I can't believe you were really here on assignment with the FBI."

"It's all crazy, isn't it? That's why I had that picture of Breckenridge. I still can't figure out why I had the pictures of your boss, however." A frown tugged at her lips. "I'm not sure if that memory is still tucked away somewhere or what . . ."

Trevor's gaze clouded as he nodded. "Maybe the memory will return."

She studied Trevor another moment, still trying to tie up the loose ends in her mind. "Were you here because of Frederick?"

"I originally came to the area because of him," Trevor explained. "I suspected he still had his operatives at work. But I had no idea when I met you that you were investigating him. I suppose that ultimately it was Frederick Moreau that led us both to this area."

"Something good that came out of all the bad." She squeezed his hand.

"Yes, you can say that again." Trevor beamed as he glanced down at her then he stepped back. "I really feel like we should start this all over again."

"I would like that. This time, without any lies."

"I'm all in favor of that." Trevor paused. "Sadie, would you like to go to dinner with me sometime?"

"I would love that."

He grinned. "That makes me very happy to hear."

Her heart lifted. Despite everything bad that had happened, hope remained.

For that, she was forever grateful . . . because things could have turned out so much differently.

She praised God they hadn't. She praised God that she'd remembered the important things—the foundation of who she was.

If Sadie and Trevor had survived this storm together, then she knew they could survive anything.

~~~

Thank you so much for reading *Shadow Assignment*. If you enjoyed this book, please consider leaving a review.

Coming next: *Shadow Collateral*!

THE
SHADOW
AGENCY
Shadow
COLLATERAL
USA TODAY BESTSELLING AUTHOR
CHRISTY BARRITT

ALSO BY CHRISTY BARRITT:

YOU MIGHT ALSO ENJOY

...

LANTERN BEACH BLACKOUT

Dark Water

Colton Locke can't forget the black op that went terribly wrong. Desperate for a new start, he moves to Lantern Beach, North Carolina, and forms Blackout, a private security firm. Despite his hero status, he can't erase the mistakes he's made. For the past year, Elise Oliver hasn't been able to shake the feeling that there's more to her husband's death than she was told. When she finds a hidden box of his personal possessions, more questions—and suspicions—arise. The only person she trusts to help her is her husband's best friend, Colton Locke. Someone wants Elise dead. Is it because she knows too much? Or is it to keep her from finding the truth? The Blackout team must uncover dark secrets hiding beneath seemingly still waters. But those very secrets might just tear the team apart.

Safe Harbor

Guilt over past mistakes haunts former Navy SEAL Dez Rodriguez. When he's asked to guard a pop star during a music festival on Lantern Beach, he's all set for what he hopes is a breezy assignment. Bree hasn't found fame to be nearly as fulfilling as she dreamed. Instead, she's more like a carefully crafted character living out a pre-scripted story. When a stalker's threats become deadly, her life—and career—are turned upside down. From the start, Bree sees her temporary bodyguard as a player, and Dez sees Bree as a spoiled rich girl. But when they're thrown together in a fight for survival, both must learn to trust. Can Dez protect Bree—and his carefully guarded heart? Or will their safe harbor ultimately become their death trap?

Ripple Effect

Griff McIntyre never expected his ex-wife and three-year-old daughter to come to Lantern Beach. After an abduction attempt, they're desperate for safety. Now Griff's not letting either of them out of his sight. Bethany knows Griff is the only one who can protect them, despite the fact that he broke her heart. But she'll do anything to keep her daughter safe—even if it means playing nicely with a man she can't stand. As peril ripples through their lives, Griff and Bethany must work together to protect their daughter. But an unseen enemy wants something from them . . . and will stop at nothing to get it. When disaster strikes, can Griff keep his family safe? Or will past mistakes bring the ultimate failure?

Rising Tide

Benjamin James knows there's a traitor within his former command. The rest of his team might even think it's him. As danger closes in, he must clear himself and stop a deadly plot by a dangerous terrorist group. All CJ Compton wanted was a new start after her career ended under suspicion. Working as the house manager for private security group Blackout seems perfect. But there's more trouble here than what she left behind. As the tide rushes in, the stakes continue to rise. If the Blackout team fails, it's not just Lantern Beach at stake—it's the whole country. Can Benjamin and CJ overcome their differences and work together to find the truth?

ABOUT THE AUTHOR

USA Today has called Christy Barritt's books "scary, funny, passionate, and quirky."

Christy writes both mystery and romantic suspense novels that are clean with underlying messages of faith. Her books have sold more than four million copies and have won the Daphne du Maurier Award for Excellence in Suspense and Mystery, have been twice nominated for the Romantic Times Reviewers' Choice Award, and have finaled for both a Carol Award and Foreword Magazine's Book of the Year.

She is married to her Prince Charming, a man who thinks she's hilarious—but only when she's not trying to be. Christy is a self-proclaimed klutz, an avid music lover who's known for spontaneously bursting into song, and a road trip aficionado.

When she's not working or spending time with her family, she enjoys singing, playing the guitar, and exploring small, unsuspecting towns where people have no idea how accident-prone she is.

Find Christy online at: **www.christybarritt.com**

Sign up for Christy's newsletter to get information on all of her latest releases here: **www.christybarritt.com/newsletter-sign-up/**

- facebook.com/AuthorChristyBarritt
- x.com/christybarritt
- instagram.com/cebarritt

Made in the USA
Las Vegas, NV
25 July 2024